A big-talking bachelor's dilemma:

I'm married to the greatest woman, we have the perfect house, the perfect life...or so I told someone, to save face. Now I've got to come up with this blushing bride—fast. If I ever *were* to get married—which I'm not—I'd *never* marry that spitfire next door, Gina Delaney. Although, I have opened my big mouth, and I'm in a jam. Since she's a do-gooder, she'd probably help me out. But I'm so attracted to her, I'm not sure I could stick to a "hands-off" arrangement.

What's a confirmed bachelor to do?

Dear Reader,

Only One Groom Allowed. Those words certainly make me think. I mean, really...I don't even have one groom on the horizon, yet Dina Dorelli, the heroine of Laurie Paige's latest, has *two?!* Some things in life just aren't fair, if you ask me. Of course, you didn't. And if I were you, I wouldn't waste time on the question, either; I'd just hurry up and read this delightful book. After all, Dina only gets to end up with one of those potential grooms, and I'm sure you want to see which one.

The One-Week Wife begins Hayley Gardner's duo, FOR BETTER...FOR WORSE...FOR A WEEK! It's incredible to think that a mere seven days can change someone's life so irrevocably—but for the better, I promise you. And after you finish reading Gina and Matt's story, I know you'll want to come back for the companion book, *The One-Week Baby.*

That's it for this month. But after you smile your way through these two titles, don't forget to come back next month for two more books about unexpectedly meeting, dating—and marrying!—Mr. Right.

Enjoy!

Leslie Wainger
Senior Editor and Editorial Coordinator

Please address questions and book requests to:
Silhouette Reader Service
U.S.: 3010 Walden Ave., P.O. Box 1325, Buffalo, NY 14269
Canadian: P.O. Box 609, Fort Erie, Ont. L2A 5X3

HAYLEY GARDNER

The One-Week Wife

Published by Silhouette Books

America's Publisher of Contemporary Romance

To Cristine Grace, for being a great editor
and for believing in me. Thank you.

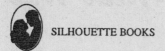 SILHOUETTE BOOKS

ISBN 0-373-52045-X

THE ONE-WEEK WIFE

Copyright © 1997 by Florence Moyer

Printed in U.S.A.

About the author

In love, opposites sometimes attract in a big way. That was definitely the case in my marriage. For instance, while I worry my head off about something, my husband will go fishing. I never stop talking, and my husband never stops listening—most of the time with a blank look and the television on. We're such opposites that even though I've always loved him, it took me a while to figure out why I *like* him so much and what we have in common.

I like him because he has a quiet sense of humor that makes me laugh when I most need to. Even better, he always thinks I'm funny—he must, because he laughs at me *a lot*. In addition to humor, we share a mutual respect. I respect him because he's smart in how things work and in common sense, and he respects me because I'm smart in everything else. Just kidding. For real, what I don't know, he seems to, and vice versa. That comes in handy.

Having discovered the above, I've come to the conclusion that when two people in love appear to be complete opposites, if you look deeply enough, there's usually a need in each that the other is fulfilling and no one else can. If that need is met, can love really be far behind? Check out Matt Gallagher and Gina Delaney, complete opposites, in *The One-Week Wife*, and see!

Books by Hayley Gardner

Silhouette Yours Truly

Holiday Husband
The One-Week Wife

1

DO ~~NOT~~ DISTURB!
Yes, this means you.

Gina Delaney's mouth twisted into a soft smile as she peeked around the tall bushes separating her yard from Matthew Gallagher's and read the sign he had posted on his tree. No wonder her new neighbor kept getting unwanted visitors!

The first had come while Gina had been trimming her side of the seven-feet-high privacy bushes dividing her yard and the one next door. She'd overheard a man—Gallagher, she'd gathered—saying sternly that he did not want to be bothered. Five minutes later, when she'd been in her garden, nine-year-old Jimmy Simmons had slipped, giggling, through a wide hole in the bottom of her bushes that she couldn't get to grow in. The child had run down the length of her driveway, never even noticing her.

About the same time, in Gallagher's yard, a rusty, masculine voice had cursed, and her curiosity had finally overwhelmed her. She'd carried her trash to the curbside as an excuse to sneak a peek into the next yard and spotted the sign on her next-door neighbor's tree.

She ought to put Matt Gallagher out of his misery and let him know someone had messed with his precious sign. But as Gina stood there chewing on her bottom lip and trying not to laugh, she reconsidered. She was an adult, and she respected the guy's original intention. Do Not Disturb. That was clear to her. Usually not even a sign like that would stop her from making a welcome-to-the-neighborhood trip to the newcomer's front door, complete with a homemade lemon cake, her specialty. But this was not your run-of-the-mill-type neighbor.

This neighbor was a *bachelor*. Eli Tuttle, their mutual eighty-year-old landlord who lived down the block, had already given her that information. And of course, he'd added his opinion that she'd be fool if she didn't hurry up, stake her claim and put the guy on layaway, since Matthew was a perfect physical clone of him—forty years removed, of course. Exasperated at another matchmaking attempt by a well-meaning friend, Gina had told Tuttle that any clone of his would be so rare he'd probably be totally out of her price range, and she wasn't even going to browse. So for her own good, Gina was staying on her side of the bushes.

It wasn't as though she was totally against falling in love again, she insisted to herself. About a year after her husband Mac's death, she'd even tried dating for a while. But after one disaster and a few mediocre dates, she'd finally come to the opinion that lightning doesn't strike twice when it comes to finding real, true love. Now she didn't date anymore. It was easier not

getting enticed when you just ended up alone, anyway. And besides, with her bridal shop, she had
plenty to keep her busy and content. No way was she
going anywhere near Mr. Do Not Disturb next door.

Walking back up into her yard, she started toward
the bushes to pick up her clippers. At that precise
second, on the other side of the bushes, she heard
Matt Gallagher's rugged voice yell "Gotcha!" There
was a sharp squeal in response, then rapidly following, Matt's voice boomed, "Ow, you little monster.
That hurt!"

Gina grinned.

Then the child Matt had apparently caught yelped,
sounding like he was in pain.

The grin leaving her face abruptly, Gina dropped
to her knees and looked through the hole in the shrub-
bery. She first saw a man with short dark brown hair
wearing jeans and a black T-shirt. Her neighbor, she
guessed. He had a viselike grip on eight-year-old
Frankie Simmons's ear as he pulled the boy toward
his house.

"Frankie!" she yelled. Both Matt Gallagher and
Frankie, Jimmy Simmons's brother, turned abruptly.
Without weighing the consequences, Gina scrambled
through the hole in the shrubs and came up on the
other side.

"Ms. Delaney!" Frankie yelled, his face pale
enough to make his freckles stand out like ink dots.
"He's about to abduct me! Call the police! Call 'Most
Wanted'!"

"You let him go," Gina demanded of Gallagher,
staying where she was for a minute while she brushed
a stray leaf or two off her clothes. Her eyes remained

glued to every movement of her new neighbor's muscular body—just in case he made the wrong move, she swore to herself. No other reason.

"So who are you?" Gallagher asked. "Their ringleader?"

Her jaw set. "He's a harmless child."

"Harmless—hell," Gallagher replied. "He *kicked* me."

"Self-defense!" Frankie protested loudly to Gina, his face earnest. "He grabbed my ear *first,* so I had to kick him. I took classes, and they *told* me to fight back."

"Self-defense, huh?" Since Gallagher still had a grip on Frankie, Gina bit back her amusement and addressed her new neighbor. "And what's *your* excuse?"

Matt Gallagher's dark eyes gave her a once-over from her feet up to her eyes, where his gaze lingered, diverting her attention from the problem at hand. His intense stare pinned her, and despite her resolve not to be enticed by any man, Gina noticed Matt Gallagher. Really *noticed* him, from his sexy, dark eyes to the way his black T-shirt stretched over his muscular upper body. Her insides began to tingle.

"I'm not looking," she insisted under her breath, digging her fingernails into her palms to remind herself to behave. Even if she *were* looking, dark and brooding wasn't her type. She preferred someone who knew how to laugh. And Gallagher appeared far too serious for his own good—or hers.

"Did you say something?" Gallagher asked, even though she suspected he'd heard exactly what she'd said.

"Yeah, she did," Frankie said. "She asked you what *your* excuse was for picking on a kid."

Gina bit on her lower lip to control her mirth. From the look on Matt Gallagher's face, you'd think Frankie was public enemy number one.

"I can't believe this is happening to me." Matt took a deep breath that made his chest expand, and Gina's tingles turned into a full-fledged wave of physical pleasure that cascaded through her. She purposely tore her eyes from his body and concentrated on his face. His dark eyes were sharp, and his mouth curved downward almost sourly. "The kid was trespassing," he said, his voice tight.

"He may well have been," Gina said evenly. "But when trespassers are eight years old, Mr. Gallagher, you send them home with a lecture. You don't manhandle them," she said, gazing pointedly at his arm. She hesitated only for a second when she saw a couple of faded scars, and then added, "And the first time, at least, you don't call the police."

That did it, Matt thought. Brother, had she misjudged him, but he wasn't about to defend himself further to this petite woman who was acting like a mama bear. His eyes skimmed her hourglass figure and her big brown eyes, and he carefully masked the jolt of physical attraction he felt for his neighbor by gritting his teeth. Any other time or place, he might have followed up on his attraction, but not here in Bedley Hills. He'd be here only long enough to get something major accomplished in his life—not to have any affairs.

"Anyway, I'm sure Frankie has a good reason for being on your property," Gina replied, absolutely sure of herself. She'd known Frankie since he was a toddler, and he wasn't a troublemaker.

"So tell me, Ms. Delaney," he drawled, "exactly what makes you think that this little monster has a good reason for anything he does?"

"Because Frankie is kind and considerate. And besides that, he's a genius," she answered, walking over and grabbing Matt's bare arm with one hand. With the other, she pried her neighbor's tanned fingers from Frankie's red ear, all too aware of the raised edges of Matt's scars and the heat of his skin. At his quick intake of breath, something inside her turned up her inner thermostat.

Growing quite warm and not liking it one bit, Gina practically threw Matt's arm away from Frankie. She should *never* have touched the man. She was twenty-seven and knew better, for crying out loud.

"Fun to Frankie is not bothering people," she said, her voice more breathless than she would have liked. "It's working at a computer or doing science projects. Right, Frankie?"

The boy looked from the man who no longer had the viselike grip on him to the lady who gave him and his friends treats on a regular basis and sometimes played softball with them. He nodded. "I was only coming to warn him that his sign would cause trouble. He scared me when he slammed through the door, so I ran."

"Sure," Matt said, not fooled for a minute. He'd been that age once. "If my sign had been obeyed, it wouldn't have caused any trouble for anyone."

"Yes, it would have," Frankie insisted. "Somebody—"

"Frankie," Gina interrupted, "that's enough of an explanation."

"It is?" Frankie asked, his eyes wide with surprise.

"It is?" Matt echoed, his mouth twisting incredulously.

Arguing further with Mr. Gallagher would be silly now that Frankie was free and had the chance to get away. "Run along home," she told the boy.

While Frankie hotfooted it down the driveway to the oak-lined street, Gina turned her attention back to her new neighbor. She'd prefer to walk away and go back to pretending that Matt Gallagher didn't exist, but then the man lifted his arm to push his fingers through his hair in frustration, and her gaze zeroed in again on his scars. They looked old, but they looked like the original wounds must have hurt. She shouldn't ask how he got them. She really shouldn't. He was a *bachelor,* she reminded herself. But her curiosity had always been a major problem for her.

"Nasty-looking scars you have there," she said, flicking her gaze toward his arm.

"Wire cuts."

"Like barbed wire on a ranch?" Whoa, if he was a cowboy, she'd better run now. Cowboys were her fantasy—

"Like barbed wire on top of a prison fence," Matt said bluntly. "That kind."

"Oh." How on earth could he get cuts from barbed wire on a prison fence unless… Oh, no. Gina backed up a step from him as a possibility occurred to her. Could he have gotten cut going over the wire? As in *escaping?* As in *from jail?*

Watching Gina Delaney's mouth drop open and her

big brown eyes get rounder than they already were, Matt was surprised at how easily the mama bear had fallen for that one. Actually, she'd been right the first time. He'd gotten cut up on a barbed-wire fence when he was a kid, rescuing his brother West when he'd gotten his pants hung up on a fence.

Gina Delaney was looking so uneasy that he almost felt guilty for scaring her. Almost. But if curvy little Ms. Delaney thought he was an ex-con and left him alone, what was the harm? It wasn't as though anyone would be worrying all that long. He wasn't staying in Bedley Hills any longer than he had to.

A good thing, too, from the looks of his lovely neighbor. Courtesy of his landlord, Matt knew all about Gina. Only Tuttle hadn't even hinted at how attractive she was. Her thickly lashed eyes were huge, brown and warm, like the eyes of a doe nuzzling its fawn. Well-rounded with a tiny waist, she had a figure that begged a man to come home to it—what she did for her jeans and T-shirt ought to be illegal. In short, she was everything Matt would like to sink his weary body into, but he wasn't going near her. He needed his privacy right now—and maybe for a long while— way more than he needed any woman.

"I'd be willing to bet the kids around here love to take full advantage of your kind nature, lady. You've got to be a pushover if you believed that kid."

"Of course I believe him," Gina said hotly. "Frankie has never caused any trouble before. He's a sweet kid, and he's gifted. He knows better than to knock on strangers' doors."

"Frankie is a boy," Matt replied, returning his ex-asperation with the neighborhood kids to the forefront

of his mind and his attraction to his lovely neighbor
to the rear. An interesting result of everything he'd
been through in life was his ability to control his emotions—whenever an emotion could slip past the iceberg that he'd become, that was.

"Boys create mischief," he explained, trying to be
patient with the woman. "That he's a genius only
means he can invent more interesting excuses when
he gets caught."

"I don't believe that for a minute," Gina said, her
irritation overriding her worry that Gallagher might
be an escaped prisoner. "Didn't you ever do anything
when you were a kid that was totally misunder-
stood?"

Matt's jaw clamped shut. She'd unexpectedly
thrown a lead brick at him. The memory of when he'd
been eleven and caught breaking into the family court
judge's office in Kentucky flashed through his mind.
Bits and pieces of that evening came back to him with
startling clarity—the glass he'd broken out of the window so he could get in; the bent, ruined drawers of
the steel file cabinet he'd pried open with a crowbar;
the files he'd pulled out while he'd searched for the
paperwork he so urgently needed to see.

Not to mention the angry faces of the authorities
when they'd caught him.

He'd broken into the office to find his little brother's case file so he could learn where West's new
foster home was. His social worker and the people at
his own foster home had refused to tell him, even
though all he'd wanted to do was visit the kid and
make sure they were treating him right. There was no
one else to care about his brother. But the people

who'd caught him had labeled him a behavior problem, and after that, no one had listened to what he
said, so he'd stopped talking.

His jaw moved tensely from side to side. The only
important thing about the event now was that he'd
failed to get an address, and he'd never seen his
brother again. That fact haunted him today more than
any label they'd put on him. Yeah, he'd been mis-
understood, but so what?

"Mr. Gallagher?"

Gina's feather-soft voice lured him away from the
memory, and he swallowed the lump forming in his
throat and sighed with frustration.

"Okay," he said, "let's forget Frankie for a minute. What about the other two kids before him? Why
in the heck is it the second I put up a Do Not Disturb
sign everybody and his sister shows up at my door?"

"What were you going to do with Frankie if I
hadn't stopped you?" Gina countered.

She wasn't going to like this answer, either. Matt
took a deep breath before he answered. "I figured he
had nothing to do, so I was going to let him pull
weeds in my backyard."

"You were going to *force* Frankie to work for you?
He's only a little boy."

"Then someone ought to be watching him," he
said stiffly. At the look on her face, he added with a
sigh, "Don't look at me like that. I *was* going to pay
him."

No one could argue with this man, that was obvious! Gina's hands went to her hips. Gallagher's gaze
dropped there and lingered. She didn't care—let him
look. Meeting Bedley Hills's newest bachelor had

only proved to her she really wasn't going to run into a love story in her own backyard—or in the backyard next to her, either.

So now that Frankie was safe, it was time she gave Mr. Gallagher back the privacy he was craving. First, though, since she was so mad at her new neighbor for being such a stick-in-the-mud when it came to children, she couldn't resist having the last word.

"If you don't want the neighborhood kids to bother you, Mr. Gallagher," she said, "you should remove the kick-me sign from your backside."

He automatically reached behind him, but stopped just short of brushing off his rear view. His lips juggled a smile, as though he wasn't used to being teased. "You mean that figuratively, right?"

Throwing up her hands in exasperation, Gina marched over his lawn to the thick cardboard sign on the tree, which she pulled free. "If you need it in writing before you understand—here." She gave it a toss that made the poster land face-up on the grass near him.

Bewildered, Matt looked down. This time his smile came fast, followed by real glee in his eyes, and then laughter that stemmed from pure enjoyment of the joke. Gina forgot herself and grinned, too. She almost, for a few seconds, saw something she could like in the tall, handsome bachelor—a sense of humor. Then, with a start, she realized how dangerous a turn her thoughts were taking. Very dangerous, if you weighed in how physically attracted she was to him.

Turning, Gina walked to the end of the bushes and around the corner into her yard, focusing on that word. *Danger.*

Gallagher had mentioned prison of his own accord, almost like he was trying to warn her away. As Gina gathered up her gardening tools, she recalled his face, his rugged features, his hardened, intense black eyes. Accustomed to seeing troubled people when she'd worked three years as a marriage counselor, she could read her new neighbor easily—he'd been through hell. He was what some people called an old soul. From the way he held his body, stiff and upright, to the way the sides of his mouth drew back, he appeared filled with tension from an unknown source. Could he be a bundle of nerves because he'd escaped from prison somewhere?

Stay out of his life, Gina, she told herself. What with the attraction factor involved, she'd only end up getting hurt. Somehow, she had to remember to stop playing Little Miss Fix-it to every tortured soul she ran across. But it wasn't easy; she'd been at it a long time.

Her need to help people had started when she'd been a child watching her parents grow dissatisfied in their marriage. As mediator, she'd read their moods and soothed troubled waters before the fights started. But her parents had grown apart and finally divorced the year she'd turned eighteen and gone off to college. The three of them led separate lives now, and all her caring had been for nothing.

That was, she thought now, the main reason she'd gone into marriage counseling. She'd been suffering because she'd been unable to keep her family together. Of course, she'd also had a knack for reading human emotions, but really, it had been her desire to prove to herself that she could be important to some-

body's life—and she didn't care whose at that point—
that had pushed her into counseling. She'd been desperate to connect, to be needed and appreciated by
someone. By saving all the marriages she could, she'd
also be saving their poor kids whose lives were, in
reality, powder kegs waiting to explode.

And so, fresh out of graduate school, she'd gone
to work at the Bedley Hills Family Help Center as a
marriage counselor. That's where she'd met Mac Delaney, a co-worker. Poor, dear Mac. He'd worshipped
her. No one ever had before, and in return, she'd
gladly given him her heart, and pretended with her
body. Finally needed, she'd been ecstatically happy
with the man, and she wanted nothing more than to
make him happy, too.

But then he'd died in a car accident. A chilly
numbness had taken hold of her body, and she
couldn't bear to return to counseling troubled couples
and see love dying all around her. Because of her
marriage to Mac, she was even more confident of her
idea that any two people, even those not that sexually
attracted to each other, could make a wonderful marriage if they remembered *love*. In love with love,
she'd opened up a bridal shop. That way she could
meet couples at the beginning of their marriages,
basking in happiness. And if sometimes she spotted
problems brewing, and occasionally gave a couple
free advice, well, so much the better for them all.

She'd been doing that for a little over a year, and
it was a joy to go to work. No way was she letting
Matt Gallagher and his *magnetism* upset her equilib-
rium and cause her to lose what happiness she was
carefully maintaining. From what she'd observed, he

didn't seem to have the capacity to care about anyone, much less *need* someone, and she knew better than to go near a man like that. Sex wasn't enough. Her parents' unhappiness had taught her that.

Closing the door to her shed, Gina walked to her patio door, flung it open and slipped inside her house. Gallagher had too many questions wrapped up around him. Where had he come from? How had he really gotten those scars? Did the answer to that have anything to do with how badly he craved privacy?

Gina stared down at her hand in surprise as she pushed the lock into place. She'd never felt the need to do *that* before. She loved her neighborhood and trusted the people around her. They were like the family she'd never had until Mac. Better than family, if you counted that she never had any arguments with her neighbors—until Gallagher, anyway. Was he dangerous? Or was she worrying for nothing?

Maybe, she thought, staring out the window in the direction of Gallagher's home, she'd be wise to keep an eye on him—just in case.

When Matt stopped laughing, he plucked up the sign with muscles toned from years of working out and carried it around to the back of his house, where he tossed it against one side of his screened-in porch. He should have known better than to rent a house in the middle of what his landlord had called "a friendly little neighborhood in a friendly little town." But he'd done without his space in foster homes and during basic training in the air force, and ever since he'd been able to afford to, when given a choice, he rented a house with a yard rather than an apartment or hotel room. Tuttle had been the only landlord around willing to rent him one here for the single month he was on military leave, so he'd jumped on it.

Friendly town or not, he hadn't guessed the neighborhood kids might mess with his sign. What he'd had of a childhood before his father had walked out on his family had been in the hill country in Kentucky. If somebody had put a sign up there, he and his brother would have left it alone.

Smiling bittersweetly, he headed into his house for some coffee. His brother West, not liking trouble, would have *made* him leave the sign alone. For sure, the two of them wouldn't have disturbed any adults if they could help it.

The old familiar tightness ached again between his shoulders as it always did when he thought about his brother. The night they'd dragged his eight-year-old brother off was the last time he'd seen West. That had been about a week after their mother had abandoned them at the courthouse, twenty years ago now.

So much had happened in those years. With his bad rep from the break-in, he hadn't been popular in the foster care system, so he'd taken to the streets. Angry with the world because he didn't have a family anymore, he'd survived on pure guts for a year until he'd gotten beaten up trying to save another smaller kid who'd reminded him of West. Bleeding, he'd stumbled into a church on Fifth Street—a place he'd figured he'd be safe—and just like that, his life had changed.

The minister and his wife had taken him in, sent him back to school and put him to work helping others. Sick of being on the streets, Matt had listened to the Cavels and channeled his anger into a relentless drive to do something great with his life. He'd finished high school and on the minister's advice had joined the air force. While training, he'd figured out what he was going to do with his life. He was going to fly, and he was going to find his brother. Once he had those goals, he'd thrown himself into fulfilling them. In the years that followed, he'd gone to college and become a pilot, but he hadn't, even with his best efforts, been able to find West.

Matt rubbed his neck until the muscles relaxed, and then he took a deep breath. His brother wasn't why he'd come to Bedley Hills—at least not directly. He was here to burn a bridge, and damn it, he needed to be alone to think. All he seemed to have done by putting up his sign was to invite trouble like a magnet—in the form of kids and Gina Delaney.

She'd be back; he knew it. Something in the way she'd protected Frankie, and in the way she'd looked at him when he'd been thinking about West, had given him the idea she was the mothering type. He'd have to be downright unpleasant when she came over again, and he didn't want to do that.

Coffeepot in hand, Matt stared down at the gleaming steel sink. Well, he'd settled into his temporary home, and he knew what his next step had to be. The question was—was he ready now to take it?

Would he ever really be?

2

Gina paced the small aisle in her bridal shop as she waited for a customer who was scheduled for an eleven o'clock consultation. Nothing had changed. Events since the sign incident had only served to make her even more suspicious of Matt Gallagher—to the point of obsessing about the guy.

If only she had time to discuss it all with her street-wise, savvy assistant, now working in the stockroom a few feet away, she thought maybe Chantie could alleviate her fears. Unfortunately, Gina's customer, Deborah Osbourne, was walking up to the shop's door, man in tow. No time.

"Ms. Osbourne's here." Gina moved closer and added, more softly, "Grab any customers that come in, and remind me I've got a problem to talk with you about later, will you?"

"Sure, boss," Chantie said, her hand waving through the open doorway. "Sounds interesting."

"It will be." Rounding the counter, Gina greeted her client, a graceful, slim redhead in her early twenties. Deborah's wedding was in about six weeks, and for this visit, she'd brought her fiancé in to help her finalize plans. Gina had long ago found that future grooms were seldom interested in details, and so, after seating the couple at the small table she kept for consultations, she directed her comments toward Deborah.

"I'm going to give you a checklist with tips to help you do everything right down to the most minute detail." Gina kept a basic list and altered it according to the type of wedding the bride had requested and whether or not Gina had been given full charge. Deborah's ceremony and reception were to be small and held outdoors, and she'd requested limited assistance. A no-brainer, which left her too much time to think about Matt Gallagher.

Taking a deep breath, she got to work. "I've got some questions for you to answer so we can get the biggest details settled," she told Deborah. "I'll note your answers on the list for your own reference later." She glanced down at the paper. "Have you decided upon your attendants' gifts?"

"I'm not sure." Opening her purse, Deborah took out the catalog Gina had given her on her last visit and tapped a page with a glossy red fingernail. "I think I want either these necklaces, or the little music boxes with the lovebirds on top." She turned to her fiancé. "What do you think?"

"Whatever you like," Joe said. He caressed his fiancée's hand, and Gina held back a wistful sigh. She missed a man's touch. She missed *touching* a man. Suddenly, she thought of Matt, and just as swiftly, she mentally shoved him and his tight jeans over a precipice into oblivion.

Deborah picked the necklaces, and Gina wrote up the order. "The ushers' gifts?"

The bride-to-be turned to Joe.

"I don't care," he said. "You decide."

Deborah chose pen sets, and then her eyes returned to her fiancé, her mouth pouting.

Trouble ahead, Gina thought. "You'll need to co-ordinate a day to take off work and get your marriage license."

Deborah looked at Joe. Gina held her breath. *Don't say "whatever," Joe.*

"Whatever," Joe said amiably.

Gina winced as Deborah daintily exploded. "Why did you bother to come along if you aren't going to give me feedback?" she blurted out, her eyes gushing tears. His face bewildered, Joe withdrew his hand from Deborah's and stared.

"I'll wait for you in the car," he said finally, rising and walking toward the door. Shoving back her chair, Deborah raced after him. The two of them stood on the opposite side of the display window, gesturing as they fought. A minute or so later, Deborah reentered the shop, still teary-eyed.

Grabbing the box of tissues she kept on her front counter, Gina offered them and waved her hand at the empty chair. "Can I help?"

Seeming grateful for the kind offer, Deborah sank down in the chair. "I don't understand Joe," she said. Taking a tissue, she wiped her face and blew her nose—loudly. "Sometimes I wonder if he really loves me."

"Only you can determine that for certain," Gina said in the same quiet voice she'd once used with couples as a marriage counselor. "But I think he does."

"How do you know that?" Deborah wailed.

"He was communicating with you," Gina said. "Women *talk* to connect, but most men *act*. The fact that he came with you to a bridal shop, a woman's territory, shows how much he cares. And he held your hand." She smiled. "My guess is he let you decide everything because what he really wants is for you to have your wedding day the way *you* want it."

"To make me happy?"

"Exactly." Gina nodded, watching her point sink in. "Do you want to go ahead over the rest of the details now, or come back at another time?"

"Another time, and I'll bring my mother. Thanks!"

That wasn't the best news—Gina had met the woman's mother. But at least Deborah was one step closer to having a marriage that might last, and that alone made Gina smile.

Waving, she watched the bride-to-be until she reached the car where her fiancé was waiting. Embracing, the two began a long, hot kiss. As Gina watched, her face heating, she flashed on Matt Gallagher's strong, muscular arms pulling her close like that, imagined one of his big hands curved on her waist and the other on the round part of her hip, right before it slid down over her buttock and then caressed—

From behind her, Chantie gave a long, slow whistle. "Whooee! What in the world did you say to those two, Gina? It's gonna take a hosing down to get them apart."

Her fantasy popping like a balloon, Gina whirled around and hoped her cheeks weren't as flushed as her body felt. Although she was pleased with herself for helping Deborah start her marriage off right, she was also kind of irritated. Marriage was so sacred, so beautiful. Lust without love was meaningless. So why was she fantasizing about Matt Gallagher, a man she would never fall in love with? She didn't need this misery! "I just gave Deborah a little premarriage counseling," she told Chantie.

"You know enough to get a man and woman revved up like that, honey, what on earth are you still doing single?"

"I've given up on finding love." Gina glanced again at the couple, who were finally getting into their car. She *knew* where they were headed, and she pushed away a wave of jealousy and longing. "Love is not in my cards."

Chantie cast a long, dark-eyed look of amusement around at walls filled with paper hearts, wedding dresses and roses, both silk and fresh, all picked out by her boss. "Yeah, sure, Gina, whatever you say." She grinned. "Just don't give up on a love life."

"I think your employer's love life is not a suitable topic for discussion at work," Gina said, grinning back.

Chantie hooted. "You're sure right about that. Your love life isn't a topic to discuss, girl, 'cause you ain't got none. And if you don't start looking around, you probably ain't ever going to get any, either."

"I don't want a sex life. I want a *love* life. I was lucky once, but I doubt if it will happen again." Even as she said the words, Gina thought of Matt and swore under her breath. She'd never melted like that before under any man's scrutiny. Everything made her think of him—and of being touched. She wanted him. But it was far better if she didn't give her body to a man who didn't have her heart—or a heart of his own. Or maybe, in Matt's case, it was both.

Chantie sorted through the mail on the counter. "You said to remind you you've got a problem?" She rolled her eyes. "But of course, I figured that out a long—"

"Chantie!" Gina scolded laughingly. "It's this Matt Gallagher again." Chantie already knew about the sign incident, so Gina continued from there. "A couple of my neighbors and I spotted him out walking around midnight, *by himself,* both last night and the night before. Everyone's edgy about that because of the minor vandalism that started this week. You add in that I'm head of the neighborhood watch and my neighbors look to me for guidance, and Gallagher is making me crazy."

She paused for a breath. "But on the other hand, I don't want anyone to report the guy to the police and get him harassed if all he was doing was exercising."

"At midnight? Cut me a break. What kind of vandalism was there?"

Gina sat on a chair opposite the counter and unwrapped a mayonnaise-free tuna sandwich from her bag lunch. "Well, two nights after the sign incident, Mr. Stephens's handsaw disappeared." She nibbled and scrunched up her face.

"Mayo-free again, huh?" Chantie asked.

She nodded. "I almost didn't wear this dress today." But she'd needed the comfort of wearing her favorite color—china blue silk—even if the dress was now form-fitting instead of drapey, so she'd left it on. "Anyway, now the saw is back."

"What did it do, go into business for itself?" Chantie asked, raising one elegantly plucked eyebrow as she opened a padded mailer holding an order of wedding invitations.

"Nobody knows," Gina told her. "Mr. Stephens found it this morning where he'd originally left it." She frowned deeply. "And Matt was out walking in the middle of the night. Isn't *that* a coincidence?"

Chantie laughed. "Just 'cause he wants to keep to himself, you think a grown man stole a saw? Sweetie, you need to get yourself a di-ver-sion. You have too much time to think, and that isn't good."

"This is *serious*," Gina insisted. "There were also dishes stolen off the Wheelers' patio. They haven't reappeared yet. And somebody broke into Jeb Tywall's rusty shed, then spray-painted words on the side of it."

"What words?"

"Paint Me."

Bursting into laughter, Chantie put down the invitations. "Sounds like you got kids running loose with a sense of humor," she said. "That's usually what it is when there's graffiti and little things missing around our block. Trust me."

"Kids," Gina repeated. Gosh, she hoped not. "But that doesn't explain why the guy goes for walks late at night."

"Maybe he's an insomniac," Chantie offered.

"He's sure robbing me of my sleep," Gina said glumly, returning to her sandwich as Chantie returned to her work. The man's wavy hair and dark looks had invaded her dreams. Loneliness vibrated almost constantly through her like a lyric from a sad song, and all because Matt had reminded her with a look days ago that she was a woman without a man.

Like Chantie had minutes before, Gina glanced around at the lace, the roses and the crystal wineglasses on display. The business was the hearts and flowers she gave to her soul. Seeing couples in love kept the tiniest hope alive deep inside her that someday real love would find her again. But after over a year in the bridal shop business, the hearts and the flowers seemed meant for everyone else but her.

Damn Matt Gallagher anyway. She'd been happy until the day she'd met him. *Was* he a criminal, or did she just want some reason to keep picturing his broad shoulders, muscular arms and searing looks in her mind over and over?

"Face it, Gina, he makes you hot," she muttered. But that didn't matter, since she didn't want a man and sex without love, and she and Gallagher were total mismatches. *He* was the no-trespass type. *She* organized neighborhood watch meetings, baked cookies for kids and had hired an assistant she didn't need, all because after years spent as a lonely, ignored only child, she hated the idea of being by herself. And now Matt Gallagher was making her wonder if, no matter how many friends she had, she'd ever feel complete without a man to hold her. Ridiculous!

"I guess I do need a diversion," she told Chantie. "But first I have to find out who's vandalizing my neighbors."

"That *is* a diversion. But how are you going to do that?" Chantie leaned over the counter on her elbows.

"I already held an emergency neighborhood watch

meeting yesterday. We're stepping up our lookout with all-night shifts. My turn's tonight.''

"Saturday night, and you'll be sitting in your yard with a pair of binoculars.'' Chantie shook her head in disgust, but then her eyes lit up. "Say, you'll have to keep your eyes on this Gallagher, won't you?''

"Among other things,'' Gina said, blushing because she already had been.

Chantie noticed. "Uh-huh!'' she said, fanning herself with her hand. "I knew it! He's good-looking and you want him!''

"All I want,'' Gina said sternly, "is to keep the neighborhood nice so I can enjoy my life. If you don't stop the bad element when it moves in, it'll just multiply, and then you can't get rid of it.''

"Now you're saying this guy is a *bad element*.'' Chantie giggled. "I'll bet that means he's real *good*. My mama used to tell me, 'The badder the boy, the greater the joy.'''

Gina tittered. "And how would she know that?''

"Danged if I know.'' Chantie shrugged her shoulders. "To hear her tell it, she was Saint Agnes and found me under a pile of feather dusters in a special room for married ladies in Mr. Ulysses' corner store.''

Gina collapsed into giggles that lasted a few seconds—until she remembered. "Uh, Chantie?'' she asked. "Exactly how *bad* can the boy be?''

"Depends,'' Chantie said cautiously.

"I kind of forgot to tell you, my new neighbor might have been in prison.''

Chantie's mouth dropped open.

"I'm not really certain.'' Gina had never felt more confused. By the time she'd finished explaining her suspicions to Chantie, the other woman was frowning, too.

"Girl, handsome or not, maybe you'd better avoid him, after all."

"You think he might be dangerous?"

"I think there's absolutely no way of telling for sure unless something happens. Just don't let your heart take over that head of yours, Gina."

"That's not going to happen," Gina protested. "I'm absolutely not interested in getting involved again."

"Oh, yeah?" Chantie uttered skeptically. "You haven't been this intense about anything since I met you. Like it or not, you're already involved in this guy's life."

Gina Delaney was following him down the dark streets of the subdivision. Purposely slowing his pace so she wouldn't fall too far behind, Matt was halfway between amused and irritated. Dressed in tight jeans and a shirt that hugged her breasts like it was a size too small, Gina would be a temptation to any lunatics roaming the streets. And since she was outside so late because of him, Matt felt duty-bound to watch out for her. But damn it, he needed to find some way to convince Gina to leave him alone.

This was the third night in a row he'd been too restless to sleep. Unfortunately, he was still too leery to do what he'd come to Bedley Hills for. Finally, after all these years, he knew exactly where his father was, had even stared at his house from across the street two nights in a row, but he couldn't bring himself to knock on Luke Gallagher's door. He was still too angry, and that alone held him back.

Had it been his brother he'd found, he wouldn't have hesitated. During the past ten years, he'd written letters and run periodic ads in a few towns around Coresburg Junction, Kentucky, where he and West had started out in the foster care system. Even after being transferred to Europe, Matt had paid a retired air force acquaintance to keep up the ads and forward his mail to him.

A year ago, the ads had finally paid off—in a way. His mother had seen one in the Coresburg Junction paper and written to him. On his very next trip to the States, Matt had visited her, hoping she would have some news of West.

It had been a tough reunion—but they had talked, and he'd learned her side of what had happened. Mary had told him that after his father had abandoned them, she'd gotten a job, which she'd soon lost. With no money and no relatives to turn to, she'd had no choice but to give up her boys—she'd thought temporarily. By the time she'd gotten a job and returned for them, he and West had been swallowed up by the system, and she'd been told she couldn't have them back. And no, she still didn't know where West was.

Matt had returned to Germany numb. To avoid thinking about how he felt, he'd thrown himself into work and earned a promotion to captain. But then his mother had written him something that had brought him here, to Bedley Hills, Ohio. His father had written her. An ex-alcoholic, Luke Gallagher wanted to straighten out his life. To do that, he was trying to find and apologize to the people he'd hurt—make amends, if he could. One of those people was Matt.

All Matt could think now was that his father was a few years too late.

His lips set in a fine, tight line, he rounded the outside edge of a privacy fence bordering a corner lot and waited for Gina. After he saw her home safely, he would flat out tell her to leave him alone. He needed to concentrate on how to handle this meeting with his father, and he couldn't do that with this mama bear following his every move. It was bad enough he kept thinking about her at the damnedest times—about how it would feel to hold her…to kiss her. Since the afternoon she'd slipped through their mutual hedge, she'd been distracting as hell.

"I am not involved in his life," Matt heard Gina say as she approached. "No matter what Chantie says, I am not involved in his life—"

His life? Gina had a crush on him? Damn, this was worse than he'd thought. Now he'd never shake her loose. Matt watched Gina step off the curb, stop and stare in confusion up the street as she realized he wasn't there.

"Are you looking for me?" he asked, stepping forward and crossing his arms over his chest.

Squealing in fright, Gina whirled and pointed her flashlight, spotlighting him in its dim yellow glow.

"Your batteries are dying," he noted.

"What are you doing walking around alone at this hour?" she asked, leaving the light on.

"None of your business," Matt said. He couldn't help but stare at the two buttons that held her shirt together over her breasts with a lick and a prayer. All she had to do was fling her arms open wide...

"It *is* my business." The light wavered as Gina gestured with her arm and Matt gulped. "I'm head of the neighborhood watch, and we've had vandalism in the area."

"All the more reason you shouldn't be out in the middle of the night alone," he said. "See how easily you could get trapped by some vicious animal?"

"The only predator I've seen since I left the house is you," she said.

As soon as she said that, Matt took another step forward, sank his fingers into the softness of her shoulders and swung her shapely body against his before she could lurch away. For a second she stared up at him, her big brown doe-eyes defiant.

"Don't you dare," she warned, but she didn't pull away.

Matt had only meant to show Gina how vulnerable she was, but suddenly, now that he had her so close he could feel her heart pounding, his own defenses were slipping away. Gina was so soft and warm in his arms, and it had been so long since he'd held a bit of heaven, that he couldn't resist. Leaning down, he kissed the soft curves of her lips. Her mouth trembled, and then her lips parted and pressed against his. The flashlight thumped against the sidewalk and rolled with a scraping sound into the street. Gina's hands tentatively slid up his arms, and Matt got the distinct impression they'd both been waiting for this moment to happen.

Matt lived for the exquisiteness of the moment, relished the feel of Gina's hands squeezing his shoulders

and running down the length of his chest. With his
tongue, he deepened their kiss, caressing the smooth,
warm skin of her neck with fingers that almost trembled as he touched her. Normally he didn't find short
hair attractive on a woman, but Gina's looked sassy
and sexy, and he loved the way it felt against his
fingers now. An intense desire burning inside him, he
tried to remember the last time he'd wanted a woman
as badly as he wanted her.

Just about the time he thought that, Gina moved
her hands and pushed away from him with a strength
that the lushness of her body belied. Matt stared at
her, certain that her wide eyes and kiss-swollen mouth
were going to haunt him all night. For exquisite mo-
ments, he'd been able to pretend he could *feel,* that
he wasn't an iceberg of frozen emotions, that there
was no hurt residing anywhere in him. No woman
had ever been able to do that for him—until now.

"Why did you kiss me?" Gina asked.

One side of Matt's mouth quirked upward. "To
frighten you into leaving me alone."

"Well, you failed miserably," Gina said.

"Yeah." He grinned. "I could tell."

She bristled. "Until I find out if you're our vandal,
I'm going to be your shadow."

"Just don't go getting any ideas," he said, almost
teasingly. "I'm not in the market for a relationship."

"Well good, because I'm not for sale." No, she
thought, but she could probably be had. From her
waist down, Gina was literally throbbing. Damn the
man for reminding her of just how needy she was.
Double damn him. "Look, I'm reasonable. Just tell

me why you've been walking the streets, and I won't give you any more trouble."

"That kiss wasn't any trouble at all, Gina," he said, deftly avoiding the issue. "Do you really like being out this time of night playing P.I.?"

"I hate it," she said. "I'd like nothing more than to go home and go to bed."

"I'll be happy to take you there." Matt couldn't remember the last time he'd smiled this much. Talking to this woman was an adventure.

Gina scowled at him. "You'll take me home, you mean."

"Of course," he said. "What did you think I meant?"

"You can cut the act, Gallagher. I have a feeling the last time you were innocent you were probably about eight."

"Ten," he said absently. Before he turned eleven and his whole life fell apart. Her remark had pulled him out of the warm dark night and back into the cold light of reality. He couldn't take Gina Delaney to bed. He didn't want to.

Okay...maybe he did, he amended, sensing the pressure of the bulge in his jeans. But it would be a big mistake. He couldn't get involved with a woman like her, the hearth, home and kids type. That would lead to love, and love he didn't invest in. Too fleeting. Houses and land, those things never failed you. When he retired, he thought he might buy both in the middle of nowhere. Too bad he couldn't buy love, make sure he owned it forever—but he couldn't.

"I can assure you," he said as Gina finally moved to scoop up her flashlight and they fell into step side by side, "I am not behind any vandalism. I might like my privacy, but I'm not out to hurt a soul."

"Don't you care that everyone finds your recluse act strange? You'll never fit into the neighborhood if you keep acting so weird." Gina was trying to act as though everything was normal, but the truth was, her body still felt on fire from his kiss, and her lips still wished for another.

"Since I don't trust people, I don't particularly care what anybody thinks about me."

"You don't?" Gina's eyebrows lifted in amusement. "Are you aware sometimes your voice says Do Not Disturb at the same time the look in your eyes crosses out the *Not*?"

Matt shook his head. No, he hadn't been. His feelings had never shown on his face—until he'd met Gina.

They rounded a corner, and he caught the fragrance of wildflowers from her hair. From nowhere, the scent conjured up the vision of a bed of real flowers, with Gina lying in the middle, watching him—

"What are you thinking?" she asked.

"You don't want to know," he said. Too gruffly, maybe, he thought when he saw the hurt on her face. But he didn't care what she thought of him. He didn't care about anyone, and he didn't need anyone. Every time he did, he just had the rug yanked out from under him, so why bother?

"I saw you go out this morning," he said to change the subject. She'd been wearing a china blue silk dress that had clung to her curves. He'd never forget the way she'd looked when she moved in that dress.

His mouth and throat went dry, and he swallowed so he could talk. "To work?"

"To my store. I own a bridal shop called Weddings and Whatnot."

Too damn cute for words. Matt couldn't say anything, so he focused on watching the dark hollows and shadows around them. If a vandal were lurking, he wanted to be ready. He didn't want Gina to be in danger.

Gina sighed. They were back on their street, and Matt hadn't told her what she needed to know. "You walk late at night just so you don't have to talk to people, don't you?"

"Yeah, and as you can tell, it hasn't worked at all."

She pointed her flashlight at his face to see if he was teasing, but his eyes were dark and unreadable.

"Tell me about this vandalism," he said, turning away from her light. He didn't know why he'd asked, but he had.

Gina didn't know why she wanted to tell him, but she did. As she finished the part about the "paint me" graffiti on Jeb Tywall's dilapidated shed, Matt started laughing.

"I fail to see what is so amusing about an old man purposely being irritated," she said.

"I saw the graffiti artist," he admitted. "She was older, chubby, had curly, short gray hair that looked like she stuck her finger in a light socket—"

"Jeb's wife?" Gina asked. Wishing she could see Matt better under the streetlight, she stopped on the sidewalk to stare at him. "Jeb's wife did that?"

"I don't know who she was, but I swear I saw her

painting the shed when I was pulling out of the driveway one morning last week. You've got to believe me."

"But she couldn't be doing the rest...." A giggle escaped her lips. It sounded like something Babs Tywall would do. The lady had enough gumption to paint a message and let her husband think they'd been vandalized. From a counseling standpoint, that marriage fascinated Gina—it should have ended long ago.

Mrs. Stephens's front porch light flicked on, and Gina started walking again. Great, one of the neighbors might have spotted her walking with the recluse. Next, if she wasn't careful, they'd think she was in on the vandalism.

"The end of the line," Matt said when they reached her patio door. While she unlocked it, he added, "Since I solved one of your mysteries for you about the vandalism, I'd appreciate you telling your friends to leave me alone. I'd hate to have to build a moat around my house."

"Don't waste the cash," Gina advised. "The kids would cross it on rafts and ring your doorbell, anyway."

As absurd as that was, Matt chuckled.

He was so damned appealing when he smiled, Gina thought, gazing up at him, it made her wish for another kiss. "Matt, if you'd only just stop doing out-of-the-ordinary things," she said with a sigh, "you wouldn't have problems with us."

"Sure," he said, not believing that one iota. "I think I'm going to buy some stock in a binocular business tomorrow. I feel a real run coming on with everyone spying on me."

"I can't believe you're against a program that keeps the neighborhood safe," she said as evenly as she could. Why was he being so exasperating?

"I'm not, as long as it's not used to butt into other people's lives."

"Is there something about you others shouldn't know?"

"That's exactly my point, Gina." He smiled slowly. "This watch stuff is turning you into a snoop." With that, he strode away.

"I've got news for you," she called after him, "I already was!" Exhausted, she slipped inside her house instead of resuming her watch. Whether or not she would follow him again she didn't know, but tonight, she was done.

Leaning against her locked door, Gina pressed her fingers against her mouth. The throbbing inside her had died down to an ache of desire. Matt had accomplished what he'd set out to do. He'd sidetracked her—right into his arms.

Damn. Pulling off her clothes and pitching them to the rug as she went, Gina headed toward the shower. Didn't it figure? The first man she'd found the least bit interesting since Mac's death, the first one who'd reminded her she was a woman, and all she felt for him was lust. Not respect, and not trust. Lust. Worse, he was a recluse and possibly an ex-con.

She should have slapped him when he'd kissed her.

Sitting in the dark and staring through his window, Matt watched every light upstairs in Gina's house blink on. He'd thrown her for a loop, but she wasn't going to let go. She wasn't the type.

So he had to. He was thinking too much about her, how it felt to kiss her and hold her in arms that had been empty for too long. He needed to leave town before he kissed her again—or worse.

Tomorrow. Tomorrow morning he was going to that house he'd been staring at, and without a plan, without knowing what he was going to say, he was just going to do what he'd come to Bedley Hills to do—confront his father.

3

Early the next morning, Matt sat in his car in front of his father's brick house, his nerves buzzing.

Just go knock, he told himself. *Get it over with.* Then he could get the hell out of Bedley Hills, away from Gina's allure.

He hit the steering wheel. Why now? Why had he finally stumbled across a woman who might have the power to make him feel again? Why now, when he was supposed to be dealing with the issue of his father, was he instead obsessing about a woman with doe eyes and a big heart for kids?

He took a deep breath, forcing himself to concentrate on Luke Gallagher. His father's leaving was why he couldn't settle down, why he stayed busy...why he stayed apart from the world. If he could get his past settled in his mind, maybe he could finally have a normal life.

It was time. The next minute rushed by in a blur as he got out of his car, walked up the driveway and rapped on the front door. Seconds later, it opened, and time stood still.

Thinking and dreaming about this moment for almost twenty years was one thing, but now that Matt actually faced his father, he didn't know what to say. They had the same hair color, so deep a brown it was hard to tell it from black, but Luke's was graying now. His father also had his build, broad shoulders and a still-flat midriff, even though according to Matt's mother, Luke was sixty.

"If you're a salesman or a con man, you might as well save your breath. I haven't got anything worth a nickel anymore," his father said, traces of Kentucky in his speech.

"Isn't that the truth," Matt agreed, even as he fought hard against the clench of sympathy in his gut. He didn't want to feel anything for his father, because that would mean he cared about the old man, and he didn't care. Why should he? His father hadn't cared two hoots for his kids or his wife.

Luke Gallagher apparently thought a crazy man had chosen to bother him today. Suddenly looking alarmed, he stepped back to close the main door. Reaching out, Matt jerked open the screen barrier so he could see the man's face clearly.

"No, don't go. It's me, Matt."

"Oh, my God." Luke's face filled with shock, but then a ray of hope filled it. Again, Matt had the sensation that he was about to kick a dog when it was already down, but he fought against his guilt by remembering his little brother's face as they tore the kid away from him and left both of them with nobody. No real family for almost twenty years.

"Come in, Matt. Please, come in." Luke swung the door wide open. Once Matt stepped over the threshold, Luke started forward as if to hug him, but Matt drew back, purposely putting off the gesture. He hadn't hugged anyone for years; he saw no reason to start with his father.

Luke jolted backward, but then nodded slowly as though he understood, and then waved toward the couch. "Please, son, sit down."

Ignoring the "son" part for now, Matt nodded. He'd sit, he'd talk, and he'd get the answers he'd been waiting years for. Why had Luke left? Why had he robbed him and West of their youths? How could anyone walk out on their children like that? After Luke told him, he planned on walking out and not looking back.

Surveying the small living room, Matt maneuvered around a cluttered coffee table to sit on a worn-out couch. From what his mother had said, his father had just moved to Bedley Hills late last year from elsewhere in the state. Where Luke had been before now, his mother either hadn't known or hadn't wanted to say.

Matt's anger began to boil inside him. He wanted to yell at his father for leaving them on their own; he wanted to tell his father about living on the streets and about the bitterness inside him that wouldn't go away. But on the other hand, he didn't want to give Luke the satisfaction of finding out his leaving had so much power over his son that it had destroyed Matt's chances of trusting people and of feeling emotions that ought to come naturally to a person.

"Hold on, son. I'll get us some coffee," his father said, disappearing into a hallway.

Staring around the nondescript, working-class living room, Matt shoved his hand through his hair in frustration. It was finally payback time, and he didn't have the slightest idea of where to begin.

His father returned with two thick white mugs filled with coffee, one of which he handed to him. Matt held it for a minute, letting the heat burn into his palms and center him. He could handle this. Hell, if there was one thing he'd learned, it was that he could handle anything. One step at a time.

Luke smiled tentatively, as though afraid he might make the wrong move. "I know you have a lot of questions."

"Yeah," Matt said. "One right after another. Mom sent me your address, but she wouldn't tell me where you'd been or why you'd left. She said I should come see you and ask."

Luke nodded. "Mary's still angry with me, but she did write and tell me she'd talked to you. She wasn't sure if you'd come. I had almost given up hope."

"I didn't figure there was any hurry to get here," Matt said. "It took you almost twenty years to contact Mom. You could have written me." *With an apology.*

Luke cleared his throat. "Your mother didn't want me to push myself on you, so she wouldn't tell me where you were. Son—"

Matt shook his head. "I'd appreciate it if you'd stop calling me that. Matt's okay, but let's not pretend a relationship that hasn't existed for a long time."

His father bowed his head, looking ashamed. Matt shifted uncomfortably. "So I'm here," he said. "Why did you leave us?"

Leaning forward, Luke picked up his coffee mug with shaking hands. Since he was taking his sweet time about answering, Matt stared around him. The walls were bare. No paintings or photographs of his family. Had Luke left without taking so much as a picture of his sons? Or had he purposely wiped them out of his life altogether?

"I drank." Luke said finally. His eyes were the same intense ones that Matt saw in the mirror every morning when he shaved. "Your mother told me to choose—the bottle or you boys and her—and...I chose wrong." Stopping, he shook his head. "It was solely my fault, and I am very, very sorry."

"Hmm," Matt said. Even with the coffee mug warming his hands, and the coffee heating his throat and stomach, he still felt icy cold around his heart.

A picture of Gina drifted into his mind, bringing with it a surge of warmth. He shouldn't have been so hard on her. They were so dissimilar, she couldn't possibly understand what drove him....

"I'm sorry you're so unhappy," Luke said, jerking him out of the comfort of his thoughts about Gina.

Momentarily confused, Matt frowned. "Unhappy?"

"Your mother told me that things had turned out awful for you. That you'd never married, or anything. I'm sorry. You boys were the most wonderful things that ever happened to me, and I was a fool to give you up for liquor. That finally hit me two years ago, when I started straightening out my life."

Abruptly, Luke stopped talking and shook his head. "But I'm not the important one here, Matt. You are. I wish I could help you somehow—"

"I don't need any help," Matt said icily. God. His father thought he was a basket case. He certainly didn't want his father's pity, nor did he want his father to know the man's leaving him had held so much importance in his life that he hadn't been able to cope with relationships as an adult. His pride was already suffering. "I'm fine."

Luke set down his cup. "But West is still lost and you don't keep in contact with your mother much—"

"She knows where I am if she needs me." Matt would never fail to come through for her. She, at least, had tried to keep the family together. Things had been hard for a woman alone back then—hell, they still were. But his father had been different. His father was a *man* and should have been able to cope.

"You're alone and unhappy...." Luke said.

"I'm not alone." Matt breathed outward. He knew his father was trying to relate to him, but that wasn't what he wanted. He wanted his father to see what a wonderful son he had and what he had missed not having Matt in his life. What he'd be missing in the future, after Matt left.

But now he had to come up with an explanation to what he had just said. The hell he wasn't alone. He was the loneliest person on earth. He guessed saying he had a pet dog he loved wouldn't cut it. That would be pitiful, and besides, if his father knew he flew off for weeks at a time, it wasn't even believable. If he were going to lie to the man, he might as well do it right.

"I have a wife," he blurted out. Yeah. That was more like it. Hell, why not?

Luke looked confused. "Your mother didn't know that."

"My marriage was sudden." At least that was the

truth. This had to be the quickest marriage on earth, concocted in less than a second.

His father's keen eyes focused on him as he waited for an explanation. Matt shrugged and added, "After I visited Mom, I went back to Europe. On the next trip back here, my girlfriend and I tied the knot."

Luke still looked doubtful. "Are you and she having problems, Matt? Is that why you never told your mother?"

"No problems at all," he said, shrugging nonchalantly. "I just didn't get the chance to send out notices. I'm not much on writing, and I had to fly off again soon after the wedding. I'm in the air force," he added, feeling a great need to change the subject from the wife he didn't have. "Did Mom tell you that?"

"She said you fly fighters."

"That's right." Matt stood and stared his father straight in the eyes. "Got myself through school, love my job, love my wife. All I need is to win a Purple Heart or a Medal of Honor, and I'll be a regular red-blooded American hero. So you can rest easy. Put any thoughts you might have had that you wrecked my life out of your mind. I did real well without your guidance, and I suspect I'll continue right along down the same road I've been on." *Wasn't that the truth, too?* "Since I don't need you, I suspect it's time we parted ways again."

His father winced, and as he stood up, his face held a look of regret and sadness so strong that Matt once again felt strange inside. For so long, he'd waited to meet up with his father, and now that the meeting was almost over and he had his answers, it didn't feel as if anything had changed for him. He still felt angry. But there was nothing left for him to say.

Luke, however, had plenty. "I don't believe you, Matt. I think everything's the same as when you talked to your mother. You just don't want me to worry about you."

"You're questioning me?"

"I'd like to meet this wife and see for myself that you two are happy," Luke said.

Matt wanted to say no. But if he walked away, and Luke forever believed he was lying, he wouldn't have proved to his father that his leaving hadn't affected him adversely. Matt wasn't sure why it was so important to him, but it was.

"Fine," he agreed stiffly. "Right now, she's visiting her parents in New York. Just as soon as I can get her here, I'll bring her over, and you can see for yourself just how well my life turned out. I'll be in touch."

Without waiting for his father to say another word, he crossed the room, pushed through the screen door and strode down the driveway to his car. He was just getting in when he heard his father call from the house, "You didn't tell me her name!"

You'll know when I know, Matt thought, shutting the door and pretending he hadn't heard his father's voice. He wasn't certain how he was going to get a woman to pose as his wife for a day, but he supposed he could go to an employment agency or put an ad in the paper. Once his father saw a warm and loving woman in his arms, maybe Luke would believe his older son was just fine. And then, Matt thought, he could walk away and stop wishing for what couldn't be—a real family relationship with his father, mother and brother. It couldn't be, because until West was located, he wouldn't be able to forgive his father totally. Maybe not even then.

As he drove away, he flashed on asking Gina to volunteer, but immediately shook his head. Doing so would cause more problems than the solution was worth. It was bad enough that he'd already kissed her; if he approached her on this, Gina would start thinking he was interested. Besides, he didn't need her help. After all, how hard could it be to find a woman to pose as his wife?

As it turned out, more was involved for what he wanted to do than Matt had first imagined. That day, as he composed the ad, something occurred to him. What if he found a woman in Bedley Hills and it turned out his father knew her? The odds were against it, Matt knew, because the town wasn't that small, but just in case, it would be pathetic if Luke caught him in a lie. He decided to stick to advertising in the next town over, twenty miles away.

And then there was the pay and the amount of time the job would last. What he ended up with was simplistic:

Woman in twenties wanted to play wife for up to one week. Legitimate work. Pay rate $100/day, one day minimum.

He'd ended it with his first name and his phone number. He put in the one-day minimum because he figured it would take a half day to rehearse the back-

ground story he'd prepared that morning, and a half
day to convince his father he was happy. But with an
indefinite time frame, Matt could keep his options
open. He didn't really expect it would take any longer
than a week, tops, to convince his father he had a
marriage made in heaven.

The ad went into the paper the next morning. In
the following two days, Matt had five calls. One
woman turned down an interview when Matt had told
her the job was on a private basis and not in a theater
production. After that, he'd held back that particular
bit of information. Two women had been over forty-
five but hopeful—and he'd gently told them that it
was a very specialized role. A vast age difference
between Matt and his wife would give his father new
worries about his happiness.

That left two interviews. The first was scheduled
for a few minutes from then at three—Marcia Peter-
man. If all went well, Matt would cancel the other
one and spend the rest of the afternoon rehearsing.
Then he and Marcia could visit Luke tomorrow. After
that, he'd be free to fly somewhere exotic to relax
until the rest of his leave was over.

While he knew he ought to be happy that he was
so close to leaving Bedley Hills, he couldn't stop
thinking about Gina. She had pretty much left him
alone since their last meeting. While he should have
been pleased, for some reason, he kept wondering
why he no longer warranted her attention. Whenever
he went outside lately, he found himself looking
around, half expecting her to pop up. She didn't, but
he still felt like someone was watching him.

A car pulled up into his driveway blaring music

loudly enough to make Matt wince. If there was anything he valued as much as his privacy, it was quiet.

The music stopped abruptly. He stepped out onto the porch at the same time his first interviewee tottered up the sidewalk on high heels. Almost reflexively, he reached out to help her up the porch steps.

"Hi! I'm Marcia."

Red-haired Marcia seemed awfully young, with a black leather miniskirt and a bad perm. She was about five feet, if you counted the two inches her teased up, hairspray-stiffened bangs added. Matt didn't think he could bear to touch her hair, let alone an arm or a shoulder. And if he didn't touch his "wife," his father would see through his ruse in a second.

"You *are* the one who had the ad?" she asked when he didn't speak. "Matt?"

"Exactly how old are you?"

"I turned twenty yesterday."

Matt quirked his eyebrow and stared down at the girl. Just twenty appeared awfully young. So young, in fact, he felt awkward even talking to her. He didn't want her—or anyone else who might see her here— to get the wrong idea.

He'd never be able to pretend he was happily married to this woman, and that was the whole idea of hiring someone. If he couldn't pull off the pretense, his father would just pity him either for his choice of wives or for having to lie about his happiness. Matt wouldn't be able to stand that.

Marcia was looking up at him, and then, suddenly, her eyes narrowed suspiciously. "Why aren't you saying anything? You aren't a prevert, are you?"

"That's *pervert,* and of course not."

"So what's the play we're doing?"

"No play. I just needed someone to pose as my wife for an afternoon." He didn't see the point of explaining anything beyond that to her, since he'd already decided that she wouldn't do at all.

Marcia gave him a long, assessing look as she flipped her hair back over her shoulder. "Why did you have to advertise? Somebody who looks like you ought to have women lined up at your door ready to help you out."

"I'm new in town." At least he didn't have to lie.

Her giggle sounded like the high-pitched mew of a hungry kitten. He shook his head. "No offense," he said, "but I don't think I can hire you."

"Men," she muttered under her breath and turned to go. Remembering how shaky she was on her heels, Matt offered his forearm to help her off his porch and to her car. He didn't let go of her until she was holding on to the car for balance.

"Thanks," she said brightly. "I usually live in running shoes. This is just my glamorous image." She tugged at her miniskirt.

"I'm sorry this didn't work out."

"That's all right." She turned to smile at him. "You're a little over the hill for me, anyway."

Over the hill? He was only thirty. Before he could reply, he heard the rustling of branches in the shrubs. Glancing past the car, he didn't see anyone, but that didn't mean the bushes didn't have ears.

"At least you didn't try anything funny," Marcia added. "My mother was worried about that."

Oh, Lord, Gina was going to have a field day with this. But there was nothing he could do. "Tell your mother you're really safe in this neighborhood," he said loudly. "Believe me, I can't get away with a damned thing around here."

Marcia shot him a strange look and hurriedly slipped into her car. She shut and locked the door, then turned her music back on. Matt stepped back as she gunned the motor and screeched out of his driveway, leaving an impression on the concrete and absolutely none on him.

Shaking his head, Matt stared down at the same hole in the shrubs that Gina had wriggled through when he'd had Frankie in his grip. He caught a glimpse of her face for a second before she pulled back and disappeared from view, and then he heard her soft laughter.

Irritated, yet unable to keep away from her, he strode to the end of his driveway and up the length of hers. Sure enough, she was sitting on her patio reading the newspaper. She was in shorts and a clingy sleeveless knit top. All he could think of was that she had the softest-looking shoulders he'd ever seen—and one of them had a tiny green leaf on it.

He reached over and plucked up the leaf, ignoring the electricity he felt inside when his fingers touched her skin. Static, he told himself. Nothing more. "Don't you have anything better to do?" he asked, showing her the leaf.

Gina set down her paper and stared at him over her sunglasses, her rosebud mouth curving in a smile that set off sexual impulses inside Matt.

"I would have come over to your house to ask you about your visitor," she said sweetly, "but you warned me you didn't want to be disturbed. Or did you forget?''

"Did it ever occur to you that my visitors are none of your business?" He wanted to kiss her, and that irked him.

"Who visits you *is* my business when somebody blares music that disturbs my peace." Gina tilted her chin defiantly. "I was just checking to see if I'd have to come over and ask you two to settle down. But your little friend was leaving, so I decided against bothering you." She slipped off her sunglasses and put them on the table. "Really, Matt, she hardly seems your type."

"Thank you," he said gratefully.

Gina frowned. "Is she your sister, then?"

"No." A look of pain flashed over Matt's face, bringing Gina to her feet, uncertain at why he should show vulnerability over such a simple question.

"You don't have to be embarrassed, Matt. She wasn't *that* awful."

"I only have a brother." In the next instant, the hurt left his features. "And who *she* was is none of your business, Gina. Keep your pretty little head out of the bushes, would you?"

"You're just irritated because now not only are you weird—you're also over the hill." The concern on her face changed into a pert, knowing smile.

"Wrong." With a suddenness that startled them both, he pulled her into his arms and kissed her. He meant it to be a brief kiss to remind her that she knew damn well he wasn't over the hill, but it turned into something more, something hot and powerful that he wished would last forever. Kissing Gina made him feel on top of the world, as if he could handle anything—even his inner pain over his empty life.

Pulling her more tightly against him, he continued to kiss her. She pressed into him, and he felt himself harden instantly as his fingers wandered under the confines of her top. The intimacy of touching the bare, soft flesh of her back started a throbbing in him that begged for relief, and Matt knew he had to stop now. He was empty, hardened, cold—not the type of man Gina needed.

Stepping back a couple of feet, Matt gazed at her, struggling to recover his wits, but it was hard as he watched her cleavage rise and fall.

"So am I over the hill or not?" he demanded.

"Well..." Gina paused. "Your friend did seem a bit young to make that decision. I'll have to admit, maybe she wasn't fully developed yet."

"I didn't notice," he admitted.

"You *are* getting old." Gina chuckled.

"I don't think so. I noticed you were fully developed the second I saw you."

Gina felt lost in Matt's gaze. Suspected jail escapee or not, he was a damned seductive man. Not only was he darkly handsome, he knew how to kiss, and he knew how to hold a woman with just the right amount of pressure that left her yearning for more. The feminine part of her was flattered that he seemed to want her so much, but then again, he was turning into such a *problem.* Now she had to decide if she *wanted* his attention, and she didn't know. She just wasn't certain she needed to get involved with a man who was so...remote.

"If I told you I'm interviewing women to do a job for me, would you stop spying on me?" Matt asked.

"What kind of job?"

"Nothing illegal."

"Well, you should know the difference," she muttered, thinking of how he had possibly been in prison.

"What?"

She blushed, a little embarrassed that he'd heard—but not much. "C'mon, Matt. That girl was hardly a gardener or housekeeper type."

"I don't want to get into it."

She shook her head. "Sorry. You're still mysterious and weird, and this is still my neighborhood. I have to keep it safe. Until I know who you really are and what you're up to, I'm going to watch out for my friends and neighbors."

Matt was irritated again. Attracted as he was to Gina physically, he couldn't think straight when he was around her. And he needed to be able to think about what he was doing. That'd be damned hard, if Gina was going to tag along after him. But what he was up to was none of her damned business, and he wasn't giving in.

"I don't owe you any explanations," he said gruffly.

"Then I don't owe you any concessions," she shot back. "And don't kiss me again."

"Not even if you beg me to." Turning, he strode away from her.

Gina plopped down in her seat and hugged her arms over her chest, trying to ignore the way her breasts still ached for his touch. This was even worse than before. While Matt had been holding her, all her defenses against him had dissolved like sugar in hot water. He was a lure she couldn't turn down—she'd wanted him to take control of her, to pick her up and carry her off. She'd felt like a ball of pure sexual energy, ready to explode if he took her to bed.

Never, ever, had she felt like this with Mac, and that frightened her. She didn't want to feel this kind of attraction to a man who was an escaped criminal at worst and just plain secretive and uncommunicative at best—the type of man she'd never be able to love. What was happening to her?

Slapping the arm of the chair she was in, she leapt to her feet. She'd let Matt be for too long. She had to figure out his secret, and when he was no longer the mystery man, maybe some of his sexual power over her would be gone. At least she hoped so, because there was no future for her with a man like Matt Gallagher.

4

This woman had to work out, Matt thought. The interviewee sitting across from him was practically his last chance, the only call he'd had during all of Thursday. She'd been hesitant on the phone but had turned out to be, so far, perfect, so he'd invited her to dinner to rehearse their stories.

A good thing she seemed promising too, since he'd run out of choices. The woman he'd interviewed after Marcia, upon hearing what the job entailed, had refused to meet with two men in a house alone. There were a lot of crazies in this world, she'd said, and if he thought he was putting one over on her like that, he was one of them. Matt hadn't tried to change her mind. He'd gotten three calls on Wednesday, but two were again too old. The third had taken one look at him and started hinting that she'd like to bear his children, beginning right away. That, of course, was out. There *were* a lot of crazies in this world, Matt thought.

At eight in the evening, the restaurant he'd chosen in downtown Bedley Hills wasn't that busy. Their booth was secluded, separated from the next by bushy potted plants on a head-high shelf. Tisha, a classy-looking blonde with style, ran an at-home business, but also worked odd jobs for extra cash. Well-spoken, she was also an acceptable age. Hoping she would work out, Matt gave her a long, serious look. "I suppose you're wondering why I need a wife?"

Hidden from view in the next booth, a shocked Gina almost spit out the soda she'd been sipping. She'd been spying on Matt when Tisha—who was so skinny Gina had dubbed her the Blond Breadstick— had shown up at his house. After the two had talked and gotten into separate cars, Gina had followed them and asked the waiter to seat her in this booth behind theirs—so Matt wouldn't spot her.

Since Matt was just on the other side of the divider, Gina could hear him better than she could Ms. Breadstick, who spoke softly. Matt wanted a wife? A wife! Well, if that didn't beat all. Was that why he'd kissed her? Had he been secretly auditioning her and she'd failed? But he'd interviewed the redhead and Ms. Breadstick, and he hadn't kissed *them*. This didn't make any sense.

But they were talking again, and Gina concentrated on what Matt was saying.

"My father walked out on my mother, my brother and me when I was ten. We hadn't heard from him until he wrote to my mother last year. I was in the air force in Germany and just recently was able to get free to contact him."

Even though a part of Gina immediately melted upon hearing about his father's deserting him at such a young age, the rest of his story irked her. In the air force! And he'd led her to believe he'd escaped from prison. She should have known Matt had been stringing her along to get her to leave him alone.

She took a sip of soda to calm down, but the longer she listened, the more infuriated she became. The Breadstick had gotten more information from Matt in five minutes than Gina had managed to pull out of him in more than a week and a half. He had thoroughly resisted her charm—while she'd been totally unable to resist his kisses. And she called herself an expert with people!

Her waiter showed up just then with the piece of chocolate cake she'd ordered. Diet or not, she'd *had* to order the cake. Therapy. She'd heard chocolate produced some chemical that soothed the brain, and, dealing with Matt Gallagher, she figured she needed it, calories or not.

There was a lull in the conversation next to her as the waiter took care of Matt and Tisha.

"Now, where was I?" Matt asked as the waiter left. "Oh, yeah. To prove the point to my father that his leaving hadn't mattered to me, I got carried away in my description of how well I was doing and mentioned a happy marriage that I don't have. My story didn't jibe with what he knew about me, so now I need a wife to show him. I've put him off for almost a week, but time's running out."

Matt thought Tisha looked puzzled, as though she were trying to recall something. "Your father left your family in Kentucky? And you wound up in foster care?"

He knew he hadn't told her the last, or where he was from. Not even Mr. Tuttle, his landlord, knew. Nobody did, except for his father, mother and brother.... Had she met his brother? His heart stopped beating as he reached over and grabbed her hand. "How did you know that?"

Tisha explained, almost apologetically, "If there's a chance your father might attend Alcoholics Anonymous meetings here in Bedley Hills, I think I met him there."

Matt let go of her hand. His father did claim to be a recovering alcoholic. "He very well might."

"His name is Luke, right?" She waited for his nod. "Now I'm certain. Luke, at AA, told us his story a few weeks back. Everything you've said is exactly what he told us. Walking out on his family, losing his two sons, and then finding out only a while ago that you and your brother had grown up in foster care instead of with your mom. Matt, he was so sorry, and so full of regret—" Seeing the look on Matt's face, she stopped suddenly. "I guess you don't want to hear this."

Matt shook his head, not trusting himself to say anything about his father. At least Luke hadn't been lying about straightening out his life. "So he's been attending meetings regularly?"

"He first came in October. Every Thursday night that I've gone, he's been there. You get to know the regulars, you know?" she added softly.

Matt nodded. She was a recovering alcoholic. Like his father. He himself had never bothered with drinking, since losing his wits hadn't ever appealed to him. Besides, he had escaped his past just fine.

"I have a lot of clients over in my city, so I've been attending meetings in Bedley Hills to remain as anonymous as possible. Your father would recognize me, Matt."

Matt sighed, frustration in every joint in his body. "You were my best bet."

"I am sorry." Picking up her purse, Tisha rose. "Look, you do what you want—I promise I won't say anything to your father about any of this. But you seem like a nice man, and so does Luke. Maybe there's some way you can come together—" She stopped and shook her head at the glare on Matt's face. "No, I guess not."

"Thanks for coming," Matt said evenly.

"You're welcome." Tisha looked like she wanted to say more, but with a shrug, she walked off.

How damned unlucky could he get? Matt asked himself. Tisha would have been perfect, and he had, unless he'd been left a message on his answering machine, no other choices—

"She would have been all wrong for you."

Oh, no. Surely Gina wouldn't have followed him again. Not here... Slowly turning in his seat, Matt saw his neighbor's face through the small gaps between the plants.

"You like leaves so much," he said, not smiling, "maybe you should take up landscaping."

"Can't. I like people more, and there isn't enough time in the day to tackle everything." She smiled brightly. "Though I must admit I'm a pretty good gardener—"

He shook his head slowly. "This is clearly just not my day," he said. "I don't believe you, Gina."

"Really, she *would* have been all wrong—"

"No, I mean I don't believe you followed me

here." He scowled. "You must have been hell on your brother's dates."

"I was an only child."

"Well, *that* certainly explains why you like to get your way all the time." He motioned for her to come around the barrier. He knew why he was giving in to her—he was discouraged, and he didn't want to be alone just then. Gina was good company. "You may as well join me."

Gina rounded the corner, a vision in one of those filmy, red-flowered skirts that overlaid a black under-skirt, and a close-fitting, dark red tank top that showed every curve of her ample breasts. Prepared for the jolt of attraction he felt, Matt was unprepared for the smile that lit up her face and sent a flood of warmth through him.

She slid into Tisha's vacated seat just as the waiter returned with drinks, his eyebrow rising in question when he saw Matt's companion had changed. Once they'd straightened everything out, they were left with Gina's and Matt's checks and a couple of glasses of iced tea.

Different companion, same problem, Matt thought, staring at Gina. What was he going to do about a wife? He couldn't concentrate on the question, with the scent of Gina's perfume and the sight of the small amount of cleavage showing over her top enticing him.

"Gina, you've got to stop following me," he said, sounding tired even to himself.

"I warned you I was going to become your worst bad dream until I found out what you were up to," she said.

"Yeah, well, now that you've heard everything and know why I'm in Bedley Hills, tell me the night-mare's over."

"Nope. It's just beginning." The smile left her eyes. "If you would allow me to give you a little advice about marriage, Matt, you don't exactly have the best reason for entering into one."

Matt leaned back and eyed her, holding back a smile. Gina actually believed he planned on marrying a stranger. "I suppose you know all about marriage."

"Actually, I do." Gina's lips widened into an all encompassing smile. "I earned my masters in clinical social work, and I specialized in marital counseling at the clinic where I used to work for three years. How's that?"

That took his mind off his problems for a second. "With that background, why are you running a bridal shop?"

"Because after my husband died, counseling was too depressing." She took a deep breath.

Matt leaned forward. "How long ago did he die?"

"About three years ago now. Car accident."

Her smile had fled. Matt wanted to reach out and comfort her, and he frowned at the notion. Was he starting to feel something for Gina besides straight lust? Was it compassion? He wasn't sure. The feeling was too unfamiliar.

"I'm sorry," he said instead of touching her, not trusting an emotion he couldn't remember all that well. "How come you never got married again? And don't tell me no one ever asked."

Gina held her breath at the intensity in Matt's eyes. If she was reading him right, he really wanted to know. She'd reached out to him, and he was reaching back.

"I dated after a while," she told him, "and finally came to the conclusion that true love never comes along twice in a person's life. I had my perfect mate, and he's gone, and *slam*..." Mimicking cymbals, she clapped her hands together. "That was it. Last chance for romance."

Matt didn't think she sounded like she was grieving over her deceased husband, just that she was resigned to not being in love again. He could relate. Having seen how unhappy his parents had made each other, and having dated a few women himself, he'd never felt the least little urge to trust "love." He was also willing to take her philosophy even one step further.

"I think you're right," he said. "I'd even go so far as to say some people probably aren't destined to ever fall in love at all."

"I'd prefer to think there's someone out there for everyone," Gina said earnestly. "That's why you should wait, Matt, until she comes along. Please don't wreck your life marrying someone just to prove something to your father."

"But I wasn't planning on marrying for real." Gina was making such an effort to help him, with no gain for herself, that he had to tell her that much. "Tisha was being interviewed to pose as my wife—for a day."

Gina's mouth dropped open. "You two were going to *pretend* to be married?"

He nodded slowly.

"But that's awful!"

"Why? The pretense wouldn't have lasted more

than a week, and I was going to pay her," he said
defensively, feeling like he'd said this before. Oh
yeah—when she'd confronted him over Frankie. He
cursed under his breath. He never defended his ac-
tions to anyone. Explained them, maybe. Defended
them—never. So why was he bothering with this slip
of a woman who had made herself his shadow?
"Cold hard cash," he added when she kept staring at
him, shocked.

"Money is not the answer to everything!" Gina
threw up her hands. "That kind of thinking is why
the world is in such a bad state today. Nobody takes
the institution of marriage seriously. Marriage is sacred!"

"Yeah? Go tell that to my father."

He looked so sad, so lost, like the little boy he must
have been when his world fell apart, that Gina
grabbed his hand in hers. "I'm sorry, Matt."

Her touch, and the way he looked at her, spawned
a wave of emotion that joined them together. Gina
knew that it wasn't just lust they had in common anymore. But it couldn't be love that she was feeling for
Matt—she barely knew him for one, and second,
she'd been there. She knew what love felt like, and
this wasn't it. It just wasn't.

She let go of his hand. "I know what your father
did was terrible—"

"You don't know the half of it." Matt's jaw went
rigid, and before he could stop himself, the words
tumbled out. "My brother and I were yanked apart
when I was eleven, and no one would tell me where
he was going. I got caught when I broke into a judge's

office to find the address of his new placement, and then I got labeled 'bad news.'"

"Matt, that's horrible," she whispered, taking his hand again. His fingers gripped back like she was his lifeline.

"I handled it," he said. "What I couldn't take was that I never saw my brother again, and I can't find him now. Until just last year when my mother found me, I haven't felt really connected to anyone." Until Gina, Matt thought. Why her, damn it? Why was he latching onto a woman who deserved better than a man who didn't know what love was? He had no business getting her involved in his mess.

"Oh, Matt." Her eyes filled with tears.

"Anyway," Matt said, taking a breath and gaining control, "that's what my father did by simply walking out." Reaching over, he wiped her cheek with the edge of his finger. He heard the subtle intake of her breath when he touched her, and felt the almost electric wave of energy in the air. Not wanting to look into her eyes for fear they would hook him forever, he let his gaze drop. Big mistake. The cleavage he saw that promised much more hidden beneath her top jolted him again.

He hadn't been this unable to control himself since he'd gone through puberty, for criminy sakes. Common sense told him he ought to be running from this woman. So why the hell was he just sitting here, hoping that he could work up the courage to ask her to come to bed with him?

"Don't worry, Gina. I'm not a kid anymore."

"I noticed," she said, a smile breaking through the clouds.

Matt put his hands up as if to shield himself. "Oh, no, she's flirting with me."

"I am *not*," Gina protested, but she wasn't fooling either of them. With a shake of her head that set her dangling silver earrings jiggling back and forth, she said, "You should get some real counseling."

"This doesn't qualify?" he teased.

Gina's breath caught. "Contrary to what you might think, you *are* weird, and I don't want to have a thing to do with you. I only came here to make sure you weren't a bad element in the neighborhood. Now that I know you aren't, we never have to see each other again. Besides," she added, making no move to get up from the chair, "I'm a *marriage* counselor."

"I don't need anybody telling me I'm crazy for being angry," he said. "As soon as I prove something to my father, it'll be easy to push the past behind me where it belongs."

Gina knew he was lying to himself, but she didn't point that out to him. She was too busy concentrating on the way he seemed to focus on every word she said, and the way his wavy hair looked so soft.... She cleared her throat. "So you haven't been in prison," she said. "You've been in the air force."

Remembering Gina thought he was an escaped prisoner, Matt grinned. Women loved a man of mystery, didn't they? If he teased her, let her see something in him to like, maybe she'd stick around for a while—for tonight, anyway. No longer than that. "The air force," he repeated, nodding. "That was a good cover, wasn't it?"

"Matt—"

"You couldn't expect me to tell Tisha anything

about what I did, could you? I mean, if she heard I'd escaped from prison, she might have turned me down flat."

Gina stared at Matt speculatively. Was he teasing her? Feeding her another line? She couldn't read him. The man was a total challenge to her. Maybe everything he'd said to the Blond Breadstick was a lie.

No, she decided. What he'd just told her about his childhood was the truth. There had been too much heated emotion behind his eyes for it to have been a lie. She doubted he even knew how much feeling he had buried inside him. "How are you going to continue to pretend to be married, living in the same town as your father?"

Matt was grinning, but the question made him stop. "I'm only here until I show my father how happy I am, Gina."

A huge wave of disappointment flowed over her at that news. "Well, now that I know you aren't a menace and that you're beyond help, I guess it's time I left you to your own destruction," she said, rising. He was leaving town, and she didn't care. She swore she didn't care at all.

"Please stay." Matt rose, too, and reached out to touch her arm. When his fingers brushed her skin, and the heat of his palm melded with the warmth of her forearm, she stared at him, her rosebud-shaped lips parting.

Matt wanted to kiss her, lose himself in her body, her breasts, her hips...her sweet caring. Lord, he'd never met a woman who cared about things like she had, to the point of following him all over the place to make certain he wasn't a threat to her neighbors.

"Marry me," he said suddenly.

Feeling a sexual awareness of the man so acute her arms got goose bumps and her nipples hardened under her tank top, Gina had to think about what he'd asked for a minute.

"You mean, *pose* as your wife, don't you?" she asked.

Was that what he'd meant? Matt blinked and let go of her. Yeah, of course that's what he'd meant. He nodded.

"You could ask me that after I just told you that I think marriage is sacred and you shouldn't be playing around with your life like this?" She shook her head. "Matt, you must be either desperate as all get-out or crazier than I thought. In a word—no." Turning, she walked away from him toward the exit.

"I am not desperate," he protested. When she didn't acknowledge she'd heard, he added silently, *No, not desperate.* But maybe he was getting a little crazy—crazy-in-lust to have even considered asking a woman that so attracted him to pose as his wife. He was opening himself up for trouble he didn't need.

To heck with Gina. He had nothing left to do but go all out to find a wife. It was time to ask the one person who knew everything and everybody, for help.

The next morning, in his kitchen, Matt stared at his landlord, who was unscrewing the cap on the beer he'd bought to bribe him with. How on earth had his life come to the point where he'd been forced to ask an eighty-year-old man for help in finding a woman? To say that he was getting desperate was putting the matter lightly.

"I asked you over here, Mr. Tuttle," he said, sitting backward on a chair, "because I have a problem." He waited until Tuttle sat, too, and dived in. "I need a woman."

"Heeya!" Tuttle guffawed and slapped his knee. "I knew the second you moved in you were gonna be fun, boy, and sure enough, I was right. Where should we go looking? One of those swinging places like the Lotta Lust? We can pick up a quick fix there, one for each of us and then—"

"Uh, no, sir," Matt said, sticking up his hand like a school crossing guard to halt Tuttle's stream of ideas. That was all he needed. A night out in a strip joint with an eighty-year-old man who was trying to pick up twenty-something-year-old women. They'd probably get arrested and make the front page. Then his father would find out everything, and worse, Gina would probably bail them out and have a field day saying "I told you so now get out of town."

"The truth is," he clarified, "I was thinking more along the lines of something like a wife."

"Oh, that." Tuttle sounded disappointed. "Wives aren't any fun."

Matt wondered if Tuttle knew about his friend Jeb's wife painting his old shed. Probably not, since even Tuttle had mentioned how pitiful it was that vandals kept running around making decent peoples' lives miserable.

"Not a real one," he told Tuttle. "I want to get someone to pose as my wife for a while. A woman from out of town preferably, so not many here would recognize her. I'll pay well."

Tuttle studied him with squinty eyes. "Maybe that Gina next door is right."

Matt's insides tightened. "How so?"

"She claims there's something strange goin' on with you. She's worried you might even be escaped from prison because of those scars on your arm and how you want to keep your affairs private."

"I gave you my references."

"Hell, boy, the only thing I checked on about you was that your twenties weren't counterfeit. You think I'm gonna waste good money calling long distance to make sure you really are in the air force? Not on your bottom dollar. Besides, even if you escaped from the big house, I know character when I see it. You ain't gonna wreck my house. You just plain ain't the type."

The people in Bedley Hills were bizarre, Matt thought. "If you think Gina might be right about me being an escaped con, why aren't you more worried about it?"

Tuttle chuckled. "Did some time myself back in Georgia in the forties. Doesn't mean you're dangerous."

Tuttle had been in prison? Did Gina know? Matt grinned at the possibilities. "I'm not dangerous," he told the old man. "I wasn't really in prison."

"Ri-i-ight," Tuttle said in an I'll-keep-your-secret tone of voice. "What were you in for? Bad checks?"

"Honestly," Matt said. "As for the scars, I got them when I was a kid rescuing my brother."

"Ri-i-ight," Tuttle said again.

Laughing, Matt gave up. "So do you know anybody?"

Tuttle took a long swig of beer and his gray eyebrows knitted together as he considered. "If you don't want that little girl next door, I think I can come up with somebody just as good."

"Gina's out. Can you get this into motion fast?" Matt asked.

"No problem." Tuttle grinned, showing his perfect white dentures. "But it'll cost you."

Of course. Matt nodded solemnly. That was always something he took for granted—everything had a price.

5

Gina was fuming again, but this time, it wasn't about Matt Gallagher. After checking out that there was a Luke Gallagher in the phone book, she'd driven by the address on her way home from work and spotted a man who resembled Matt sitting on the porch reading a newspaper. So it was very possible Matt was in the neighborhood to do exactly what he claimed, and as far as the vandalism, she no longer thought that he had any part in it.

No, she was furious because she'd come outside to do more gardening after dinner and the two baby spider plants she'd just potted were gone. Poof. Just like that.

The thing was, she would have gladly given the plants away if someone wanted them that badly. No one had to steal from her. After Mac had died, she'd given her heart to this neighborhood, just so she had a place to call a real home and people who accepted her. Now someone was taking advantage of that kindness, and that was one thing she didn't stand for. She felt used.

Chantie still believed children were behind it, but Gina wasn't certain she agreed, especially now that

Babs Tywall had confessed to painting her own shed. Still, the neighborhood kids were always outside, and it wouldn't hurt to ask them if they'd seen someone in her yard.

Walking out her patio door, she glanced at the hole in the bushes and wondered if Matt had found a "wife" yet. Since the restaurant episode last night, she'd been arguing with herself about posing as his wife just so she could try to help him iron out his difficulties with his father. He was obviously so unhappy, and that made Gina want to reach out to him, just as she'd reached out to people all her life.

But she had to face it, the man had nothing going for him except for his great body, his sexual magnetism and his profession—which, depending on your perspective, could be called glamorous. Great if you were shallow, but she was looking for *character*. Matt was too deep to be lighthearted, and too closemouthed for her tastes. On the surface, if that description were written on paper, she would have scratched him out long ago as a prospective match. He'd make her miserable if she got involved in his life any more than she already had. So why was she still obsessing about him, especially since she wasn't even looking for a man?

Because she kept thinking of a frightened eleven-year-old boy whose parents had both walked out on him. She'd secretly feared the same thing all her childhood—that if she couldn't keep her parents happy together, they would both leave her, too. She'd been lucky. Matt hadn't, but he'd pulled himself up and made something of himself, anyway.

That was why she wanted to help him, she realized.

She respected him. But he was a man who had buried his feelings for years, and he would have to dig them up himself. He didn't seem to have the least little inclination to do so—and Gina didn't want a man who possessed no warmth and tenderness.

Reaching the sidewalk, she stared up and down the empty street. No one was outside, which was strange, because early evening in the summer usually meant kids playing outside until dark. Turning right, she glanced into Matt's yard. Nothing stirred there, either, but for some strange reason, she got the feeling someone was watching her. Matt?

Quickening her step, she hurried toward the corner, eager to get out of Matt's range of vision and thinking that the kids could be around on the side street. Even continuing three blocks to the woods, she saw no one, not even Mr. Tuttle, who was usually puttering in his yard.

Shrugging, she started back in the direction of her house. Maybe some new action adventure had premiered on television or something. Maybe aliens had come down and swooped up everyone in Bedley Hills while she was in the shower. Maybe—she'd try again tomorrow.

As Gina approached Matt's house, a dark blue sports car pulled up into his driveway and a woman with honey-colored hair got out, killing Gina's alien theory—but then, Gina thought, looking at her, you never knew. She grinned. The woman paused to look at the house, and then at a paper in her hand, before continuing gamely up the drive.

Not an alien, Gina thought—another wife candidate. Apparently Matt hadn't listened to her when she'd tried to reason with him last night. *Stubborn,* she added to her list of his deficits. But maybe she hadn't presented her argument correctly. Maybe if she went over there and gave him some other ways to help himself—

Stop it, Gina! she ordered silently. His life was none of her business. Walking with great purpose back toward her house, she held her head high when she passed Matt's. Unfortunately, though, she couldn't escape him. All the way up her driveway to her side porch, she could hear his deep voice through the bushes. He was asking the woman if she would like to continue their discussion at the same place he'd taken Ms. Breadstick to the day before. If he ended up hiring that woman, Gina thought, he'd have to make his father believe they were happily married. How? Maybe by putting his arm around her, or sharing a kiss or two. The picture of him with the girl who had just shown up whirled around inside Gina like a meteor with a tail that tied her up in jealous knots.

Feeling jealous was unreasonable of her, Gina knew. She had absolutely no claim on Matt. She had no desire to pose as his wife, to be kissed and held by him again, not even for a day. It would lead nowhere, and she didn't indulge herself in that kind of behavior. Sex should mean something between two people, she felt with all her heart.

And as for love—she'd been correct from the beginning. It wasn't in the cards for them, no matter how her body tingled when Matt touched her. She wasn't stupid enough to think she was going to change his cold personality. Matt didn't seem capable of loving anyone. For her, that would be like living with her parents again, desperately seeking their love but never getting it. Mac had worshipped her, and now that she knew how that felt, she wasn't settling for anything less from a man.

Besides, Matt would only be using her for temporary thrills. It wasn't worth it. She'd spent her childhood being used by her parents as a sounding board and a miniature marriage counselor. Never again. She wanted real love in her life, not some warm body next to her in bed. Her lips thinned. No matter how good Matt's warm body might feel next to hers.

Resolutely, she walked inside her house, determined to forget about Matt and concentrate on getting her life back to normal. She wasn't even going to ask him if the latest candidate for his wife had worked out.

She swore she wasn't.

An hour later, Matt pulled into his driveway and parked. Turning his lights out, he sat in the driver's seat and surveyed his yard, seeing if Gina was hidden somewhere waiting to spy on him. After what he'd been through with Tuttle's interviewee, Matt wasn't even irritated at the idea. He could sense the draw between Gina and him as he never had with any other woman, and it wasn't just sexual. Gina was the most interesting thing that had happened to him in his whole life, a human puzzle, and he couldn't wait to see what she was going to do next. He highly suspected that she had planned *something*, now that she knew he was back to his quest for a temporary wife.

And she did know. A few seconds after Tuttle's

interviewee had arrived, Matt had seen Gina pass by his driveway, not looking right or left. He hadn't seen her since, so he figured she was in her house plotting some way to get him to tell Olivia Gottlieb to go home.

Only Matt had already gotten rid of her. Everything had been fine with Olivia until he'd told her his background story and then quizzed her on it. As it had turned out, Olivia was pure fluff. She couldn't even remember where she'd left her car keys, let alone what kind of plane he flew. So much for Tuttle's taste in women.

Now I'm desperate, Matt thought, finally getting out of his car. He was almost to his back door when he heard the rustling of leaves in the tree behind him.

"Okay, Gina, come on down," he said, turning and peering up into the heavy foliage of the tree, lit by the porch light. To his surprise, it wasn't Gina.

"Frankie, what are you doing up there?"

"You took down the sign and all those ladies are coming to your house. Can you be disturbed now?"

"Gina seems to think so," Matt muttered under his breath. But he could see Frankie really wanted to know.

"I still want to be left alone," he told the kid, "but I'm not going to yell at you about it. Just come down out of that tree." *Before you get hurt, and Gina has me run out of town on a rail for causing more trouble.*

Frankie hesitated. "Did you really escape from San Quentin?"

"Of course not." Matt swore under his breath. San Quentin? Boy, didn't that little tale get blown all out of proportion? He'd never thought the adults would tell the kids that story, let alone embellish it so much. He'd never thought it would get past Gina and Tuttle. Geez, did he really appear to be that much of a cold desperado that everyone believed he was an escapee? "Who told you that?"

"Ms. Delaney told my mother to keep us away from your yard because you didn't like company, and Mr. Tuttle told my mother it was because you escaped from prison—"

"Frankie, I'm a pilot in the air force. I fly fighter planes."

Frankie's eyes went big, and he slid down out of the tree and walked closer to Matt, though he still maintained a healthy distance. "Really?"

"Really."

"Prove it."

Why wasn't he just yelling at the kid to get lost? Taking out his wallet, Matt tossed a picture of himself on the hood of his car so Frankie wouldn't have to come too close to him. In the snapshot, he was in uniform standing in front of the plane he'd flown in Germany.

Frankie picked it up, studied it, and his eyes went big. "Wow. You are a pilot. So what are you doing here?"

"Lately I've been asking myself exactly that."

Frankie stared up at him. He really was a cute kid, Matt thought suddenly, what with his dark hair all ruffled up on top, and his freckles dotting his apple-like cheeks. Suddenly he wondered what it would be like to have a kid of his own. Nah. It didn't bear thinking about. It just plain wasn't ever going to happen.

"I like airplanes and jets," Frankie told him. "But my mom and dad say I should study and be a scientist or a doctor since I've got the intelligence."

What that implied about his own choice of a career, Matt wasn't certain, but he decided he'd better not argue with an eight-year-old genius. "You should do whatever you really want to do with your life, Frankie. You've got a few years to decide."

"Not really. I've already started high school courses."

High school? Matt's eyebrows lifted in alarm. "But you're only a kid. You're going to miss out on the best years of your life, and that isn't good." He might not be a genius, but he knew that much.

"Don't worry about me, Mr. Gallagher. I've got ways of compensating."

Matt stared down at him. The kid reminded him of West in a way, too mature for his years. He ought to talk to Frankie's parents and tell them the hazards of making a kid grow up too fast, genius or not. But that would be getting involved, and he didn't want to do that.

A woman called Frankie's name in the distance, and Frankie's ears perked up. "That's Mom. Gotta go. See you later."

"Just don't climb my tree anymore, you hear?" Matt called after him as the kid ran off. His eyes narrowed. His picture was still in Frankie's hand. Forgetting to give it back might have been a simple oversight, but there was also what looked like the top of a small paper bag sticking out of the kid's back overall pocket. It took Matt a minute, but then he remembered where he might have seen just such a paper bag recently—in his tool chest. Coincidence?

He didn't think so. Striding to the screened-in porch that he'd forgotten to lock, Matt inventoried the small tool set he owned and discovered his tape measure was missing, along with a small bag of nails Tuttle had left behind after doing some repairs on the porch.

His eyes narrowed. Lord, he was going to hate to burst Gina's bubble, but maybe it was better if she learned sooner rather than later that the world wasn't all cotton candy and sweet dreams. Frankie was either a kleptomaniac, or he was pilfering so he could sell items to get money, or he had some other scheme cooked up in his little genius mind. Any way you looked at it, Matt had discovered the identity of the Bedley Hills vandal, and he was going to have to let the head of the neighborhood watch know.

Now, why wasn't that upsetting him? He grinned suddenly, as he realized the reason. He was desperate for a wife, and information like this could come in very handy. If he played his ace right, he could win the lady's hand—for as long as he needed her, of course. He had no desire to go after a real relationship with Gina. She needed a man who could lavish her with love, and he didn't even know the meaning of the word.

Gina was bent over a box in the storeroom the next morning when Chantie flew in. "Oh, girl," her assistant whispered, "you have to *see* what just moseyed into the shop—a man who caught a bridal bouquet— and there's no sign of a woman anywhere near him."

A man who'd caught a bridal bouquet? Confused, Gina followed Chantie into the main shop, where she found Matt holding a half-dozen roses tied with a white lace ribbon.

"Why didn't I already know this?" Gina asked aloud.

"For you," Matt said, extending his arm.

"Thank you." Accepting the flowers, her lips tilted upward in a half smile of joy. The woman hadn't worked out. That shouldn't make her happy, but it did. "The woman I saw turned you down, and now you're desperate," she said.

"You were always my first choice," Matt said.

"*Sure* I was," Gina said. "You didn't want me as a wife until you'd been turned down by other women. How many has it been now?"

"I lost count—but I never wanted anyone but you."

Chantie's gaze had been swinging back and forth between them like she was observing a tennis match. She sighed loudly and began fanning herself again wildly. "I think I'm going to swoon!"

Concerned, Matt turned to Chantie, but Gina shook her head. Getting a chair, she pushed her assistant, who knew nothing about Matt's search for a wife and must be thinking this all pretty strange, down onto it. "Chantie, this is my neighbor, Matt Gallagher. Matt, this is Chantie, my assistant."

"Charmed," Matt said.

"Oh, honey, so am I," Chantie said. She turned to Gina. "Is this where you declare your everlasting love for him, get married and the book ends? Or is this more like the black moment, where you watch your best friend go off with him and live in nonstop regret for the rest of your life that you didn't grab him while you had the chance?"

Gina blanched. "This is the part where I consider writing out the minor character if she doesn't shut her mouth and soon. Chantie, if you want to stay and watch, you've got to keep quiet."

"Gotcha, boss." Chantie stared at them, her eyes big. "Go ahead, you two. I'm waiting with bated breath to see what happens next."

Matt studied Chantie for a few seconds. Hell, this was the craziest town he'd ever been in. A comedienne in a bridal shop, a neighborhood spy, a landlord who claimed to be an ex-con, kids who messed with signs and a wife who posed as a vandal to annoy her husband—with Gina the center of it all. He began to laugh and had to search for breath to speak.

"Do you pay her extra to be funny?" he asked Gina.

"Really, Matt, not everyone is as materialistic as you. Chantie's funny for free."

"You can pay me extra if you want," Chantie piped in.

Ignoring her, Gina occupied herself with putting the roses into a vase and thought hard about what she was going to do about Matt's request.

"I really need your help, Gina," Matt said quietly, trying not to notice the way her pale pink silk blouse draped over her breasts, or how the color added a rosy glow to her cheeks. "And since you don't like my constant references to money, I wouldn't even consider insulting you by offering to pay you for the time."

Gina stared at him in mock shock over the roses. "Matt, was that a *joke* that just came out of your mouth?"

"Occasionally, when provoked, I can come up with a zinger or two. Had my life gone differently, I might even have developed a real sense of humor to go along with my other assets."

"Oh, merciful heavens," Chantie broke in, fanning herself harder with a napkin she had folded. "His *assets,* he says. Gina, you either grab those assets, or I will. This is one man who shouldn't have to beg for a wife, let alone pay for one."

"Chantie, you have no idea what's going on," Gina replied sternly, putting the roses down on the counter. "And remember, Mr. Gallagher might just be a prison escapee. You were the one who said I should be careful."

That reminded Matt. "I know I shouldn't have let you believe that story, but really, Gina—San Quentin?"

Gina's eyes went huge. "You escaped from San Quentin?"

"Of course not. But Frankie Simmons got the idea I did from somewhere."

"When did you see Frankie Simmons again?" Gina rounded the counter and confronted him, poking her finger directly into his chest. "If you frightened that child—"

Matt caught her finger, ignoring the need that surged through him at the mere touching of her skin. "I'd be careful with the accusations if I were you. Frankie has the idea that I escaped from San Quentin, which is so ludicrous I won't even begin to discuss it. He got this idea from something you said to Tuttle, who told Mrs. Simmons. If anyone is responsible for scaring the kid, it's you.''

Since she looked properly disturbed, Matt decided to save his trump card about the vandalism for later.

"If you didn't escape from prison,'' she said uncertainly, "then what you told Breadstick—''

His eyebrows lifted in question.

"The woman you took to the restaurant,'' she clarified.

"Oh, okay,'' he drawled, a grin on his face as he took a long, lazy look up and down her hourglass curves. Her body reminded him of those ladies in the fifties movies—real women.

"What you told her must have been the truth,'' Gina said in wonder. "You *are* in the air force.''

Matt took his service I.D. out of his wallet and handed it to Gina. The identification looked valid, but she'd never seen one, so she didn't protest when Chantie, whose brother was in the army, grabbed it out of her hand.

"I'm a captain,'' Matt told her. "In a little over two weeks, I'm due to report to Langley Air Force Base in Virginia. Assuming this town hasn't worn down my nervous system and killed my edge, I'm going to be flying F-15s.''

"He *is* a pilot,'' Chantie whispered forcefully to Gina, flapping his identification. "It's just like my brother's.''

"Then why did you let me believe you were dangerous?'' Gina asked Matt, plucking the card from Chantie's fingers and handing it back to him.

"I thought it would make you leave me alone."
Matt gave her a charming grin. "It didn't work."

"No kidding," Gina shot back, but finally, she
smiled, too. Subconsciously he had wanted someone
to be interested in his life. He needed people, and he
didn't even realize it.

They stared at each other. The room became so
quiet and the connection between them so intense that
even Chantie dropped her usual quips. "Break time,"
she said, grabbing her purse and heading out the front
door with only a tinkling of the bell to signal her exit.

Matt watched her leave and then turned back to
Gina. "To answer your question about Frankie, I saw
him last night. He was in my tree."

Gina frowned, remembering the feeling of being
watched she'd gotten when she'd walked past Matt's.
Had Frankie been watching her—or Matt? Why?
"You didn't come to tell me you strung him up, did
you?"

He shook his head. "I think you know me better
than that by now. We had a very interesting conversation about me being in prison, and then his mother
called for him."

"I told his mother to tell him to leave you alone."

"I don't think Frankie ever intended for me to
know he was there." He probably wouldn't have, had
he not been looking for Gina. Reaching out, he
pushed her wayward bangs off her forehead. "I need
you to pose as my wife. Please?"

Her breath caught, and her lips pulsed out gently.
"I don't want to get involved in your life."

"I'm desperate," he pleaded. "I know pretending
to be married goes against everything you believe in,

but if you would just do this, I could leave Bedley Hills. You'll never have to see me again. Then you could go back to fooling with neighborhood watch meetings, and Tuttle, and Babs—all the important things in life that make you happy.''

Gina knew Matt was leaving whether or not he got a wife to help lie to his father. There was no future for them—not that she wanted one—and Gina saw no reason to make herself miserable by helping him out.

"I'll make it worth your while." He reached out and ran his fingers down her cheek, over the curve of her chin and down the exposed part of her neck, stopping just short of touching her breasts. Gina swallowed and took a deep breath to combat her racing libido. Or was it her heart?

"Just say no," she whispered. No to a man who could probably take her to heaven and home again with his touch. She was a fool, but she was going to say it. She was going to absolutely, positively, without a doubt say—

"I know who the Bedley Hills vandal is," Matt said.

Gina pulled away and scowled at him. "I don't believe this. You're trying to bribe me."

"Seduction isn't working." He glanced around the shop to make sure they were alone.

She eyed him steadily. "Did you purposely mean that to sound cold and calculating, or was it my imagination?"

He stared at her, realizing that she was right. And then he said something completely uncharacteristic. "I apologize. Let's just say I never learned how to relate to people really well. I don't know if I ever had the ability, or if life beat it out of me. So if I sounded cold, I'm very sorry. I need your help, Gina.''

Lord, Gina thought, she was such a sucker for a man in distress, and this particular one was pitiful. Matt didn't really need her help—he just wanted to use her. But was she really being used if she stood to gain something—the identity of the neighborhood vandal? If she saw him through this, and showed him how important it was that he somehow connect for real with his father, wouldn't he leave Bedley Hills destined for a more satisfying life than he had now as Matt Gallagher, the recluse?

She crossed her arms and tried to ignore the tingling lingering on her skin from his touch. Wouldn't he remember her for a long time if she helped him that much?

''I don't want to say yes,'' she told him.

''I didn't want to have to ask you.''

''Just so we both know where we stand going into this.''

''Of course.'' This was precisely what Matt wanted. ''I was just kidding before, you know. I'll pay you if you want. Same rate as I offered the other women.''

''I'm not like the others.''

''I already knew that,'' Matt said.

She whooshed out a breath. ''I don't want money, but after we visit your father, you'll tell me who the vandal is?''

''No seduction?''

''Get real!'' she said, emitting a small laugh that could be taken a lot of ways.

Matt was disappointed, but not surprised. Gina was

smart enough to keep her heart well out of an arrangement like this, just like he was—assuming, of course,
he still had a heart. Asking Gina to do this, he wasn't
so sure.

6

——◄——

"We'll be over at seven this evening, then?"

"Sounds good," Luke Gallagher said to Matt, holding the phone receiver so tightly his hand was shaking again. He didn't want to disconnect. It had been over a week, and Luke had given up hope that Matt would ever call back.

Matt didn't say anything else, so Luke finally had to let him go. Putting down the receiver, he walked over and sank into his huge armchair, oblivious to the talk show he watched every afternoon.

Her name was Gina. His son *had* found somebody. Once Luke met her and saw whether or not this woman truly did make Matt happy, Luke thought that maybe he could stand it if his son walked out of his life forever. He prayed he wouldn't, but if Matt did, he'd survive, and he'd understand.

Luke swept up the old magazines on his coffee table and began to clean up the place. So far, Matt had remained in touch with his mother. That was a good sign. Someday, if he could only find his other son, West, maybe then, God willing, Matt would forgive him for abandoning his family and ruining a big part of his life.

And if Matt did, maybe then he could finally forgive himself.

Matt spent more than an hour and a half with Gina getting their background stories straight earlier that day. He'd called Luke the minute Gina had told him she had the day free. He just wanted to get this whole thing over with so he could leave tomorrow. He'd already told Gina that, too, right before she'd gone home to change.

Matt locked his door and headed down his drive. Telling Luke his wife's name was Gina had felt sweet on Matt's lips. How sweet, he wasn't sure he wanted to admit even to himself, except that when he'd hung up the phone, he'd been grinning.

Boy, but he was getting carried away with this. Another hour or so, and the visit would be over. His point made, he could then pack his things and leave town, go ahead and set up in Virginia before he had to report to duty, or take a quick vacation to Hawaii if he wanted. He'd be free of his past. Maybe he still wouldn't be exactly happy, but what the hell. Except for his unceasing desire to find his brother, he wouldn't have a care in the world. Except...

Except that after he left, he'd have to forget the heart-shaped face and big brown eyes he'd left behind in Bedley Hills.

Damn, he thought, reaching Gina's door. He had to quit thinking this way. He didn't have anything to offer a woman like her. His emotions were so dried up he would make a lousy partner in life for any woman, let alone one that gave love out as freely as Gina. He didn't even remember what love felt like.

She pulled the door open before his fist hit twice, flashing Matt a huge smile. Warmth, he thought. Every time he was around her, that's what he felt.

"Exactly what are you so happy about?" he asked.

"I'm acting," Gina said through her smile, showing all her teeth. "Pretending to be happily married to you. An Academy Award performance, isn't it?"

Suppressing a grin, Matt was surprised to feel contentment take the place of his tension. "You have the strangest way of seeing things."

"It's called optimism," she said, and then she really smiled. "Okay, maybe I enjoy helping a neighbor in need."

Matt's eyes took on a suggestive gleam that took Gina's breath away. "Just how far does this helpfulness extend?"

"Not half as far as you'd like it to, I'd bet," she teased back in a light voice, reaching up to pat his cheek in a sisterly fashion. But the second she put her hand on the rough whiskers of his chin, she thought, *Big mistake, Gina.* There was absolutely nothing of a sisterly sense to the surge of desire that came over her.

Hurriedly, she dropped her hand back to her side and smiled wanly. "Be careful. A stodgy type like you can't have had a whole heck of a lot of practice at teasing, and you might find it backfires on you," she said.

"Would that be interesting—if it backfired?"

"It might."

"I can't wait."

He might not have to. The way she was feeling right now, standing next to him and smelling the pinewoods scent he was wearing and seeing that sexy, provocative look in the depth of his dark eyes, she was beginning to think she was the biggest fool around. He was obviously unattached—or he'd be bringing a real wife along with him this evening—and she was so obviously caught up by his whole persona of sexiness...

And it was also so obvious that he was slowly making her crazy.

"You look nice," he told her. She did, wearing a tailored, modest halter-top dress in black-and-white checks that set off the black of her hair and the gorgeous slope of her white shoulders. Matt suddenly wanted to take her back inside and kick the door shut. He had to swallow to keep from suggesting it.

"You look great, too." He had dressed up, with a midnight blue shirt and beige cotton slacks. She almost wished they weren't going anywhere....

Get a grip, Gina, she told herself, letting out a long breath.

When Gina sighed, the sound reached into Matt's gut, and he wondered if she was tense about the upcoming meeting, or if she was just suffering under the same sexual tension he was. She was holding a paper plate covered in tin foil, and grinning to break the tension, he pointed to the plate.

"What's that?" he asked.

"I made your father a lemon cake."

Matt looked down again at the shiny foil, feeling a pang of jealousy. No woman had ever made *him* a cake. "Why?"

"Because we're going to meet him and I'm your wife." She smiled brightly at him. "And because I never go visiting at a stranger's house empty-handed.''

"Have you ever met a stranger?" Matt asked, lifting the edge of the foil to sniff. Gina lightly slapped his hand.

"Only people who are strange." She gazed at him pointedly. "Are you ready?"

Since they'd already agreed to go in his car, they began walking down her driveway. Gina gazed at him for a few seconds, taking in every detail of the man from the waviness of his dark hair, to the broad shoulders under that shirt, to the slacks that fit him delectably well.

That he wasn't showing the least bit of nervousness about the meeting tonight didn't surprise her. When they'd rehearsed their stories earlier, she'd figured out that he was acting on gut instinct in respect to his father, because he was the type of person who found it easier to act than to *feel*. Too many years of being alone had done that to him.

Remembering the abandoned child he'd been, Gina found herself feeling afraid for him. She was worried that when he walked away from his father, he wouldn't be able to bury the emotions he'd be feeling deep enough. There was already too much intensity behind those dark eyes of his, and she didn't believe he could maintain this cool facade forever. Something was bound to break.

She just prayed it wouldn't be him.

But Matt had already made her promise not to try to change his mind about tonight. She'd seen the sense in that—there couldn't be any tenseness between them when they arrived. Of course, that had been *Matt's* rule, not hers....

You agreed, Gina, so leave him alone.

"Uh-oh. I forgot to lock my door." She started to hand him the cake. "Here, hold this—"

"Oh, boy," he said, grabbing for it, his eyes brightening with anticipation.

She yanked it back, her body melting as their fingers connected. "Uh-oh. You have the same look Frankie gets in his eyes when it comes to treats."

"Frankie, greedy?" His eyes widened in disbelief. "Surely the boy genius doesn't have a *fault?*"

"All I meant is that he likes to eat!" she protested.

Eat, or swipe food? Matt knew if he asked her outright, it might lead to a discussion he wanted to avoid right now about her wonder boy. No sense in inviting trouble when he had Gina firmly in his clutches. He grinned, determined to charm her. "If you will let me sniff it while you're gone, I promise not to eat a crumb," he said. "On my honor as an escaped prisoner."

Gina groaned.

"Sorry," Matt said, his eyes twinkling, "but I never was a Boy Scout, so I couldn't take an oath on that."

"Hmm. Well, since you took an oath—here." She handed him the cake.

"Did anyone ever tell you how gullible you are?"

"Yes, but no one ever said it like it might be a problem." Her hands on the cake, Gina quirked an eyebrow. "Are you going to make me sorry for my trusting nature?"

"I don't ever want to make you sorry for anything, Gina," he said, reaching for the plate.

Matt sounded serious, but also sincere, so Gina held the plate back out of his immediate reach and plunged in. "In that case, I have to tell you that I think this evening is going to be a mistake. What could entice you to change your mind about lying to your father?"

"That depends. What do you have in mind? Do I get to have my cake—" Matt's lips spread in a slow grin as he glanced from the cake to her eyes "—and eat it, too?"

He wasn't referring to the lemon confection caught in the tug-of-war between them. The way he was looking at her made Gina feel like she was the only woman in the world he'd ever want. That was so erotic. She suddenly became fully aware of every part of her body and began having visions of every part of his, especially when he stepped closer to her, with only the cake between them.

"I do believe I'll save my answer until you give me yours," she said softly.

"My answer is that we're going to have to be late—" He leaned over, and despite her disappointment that he wasn't calling off the visit set for the next hour, she ran her tongue over her lips in anticipation of his kiss. But then he grinned and added, "Unless you give me that cake and go lock your door so we can get into the car."

"Very funny," she said. Letting go of the plate, she shook her head. "You certainly are a challenge."

"That's why you put up with me," Matt said. "I bet you thought I was going to kiss you."

So he wouldn't be able to tell she was about to lie by the look on her face, she turned sharply and hurried back toward her house, calling behind her, "I did not!"

"You wanted me to," Matt yelled back.

That he was right really irritated her. Matt had a way of making her forget what was best for her. She dug in her pocket for her keys to her dead bolt and pursed her lips. He was just a bit too confident about her for his own good. If she didn't put him in his place soon, he was going to get her into bed in the blink of an eye.

Thanks to Gina's short hair, Matt was treated to the view of her bare shoulders when she turned her back and walked away. He swallowed back the urge to run his lips over their silkiness...down to where the low back of her dress was, and then back up again. He wanted to hear her sigh in that delectable way she had, just for him.

He opened his car door. He had to stop thinking like this. Despite the attraction between them, a relationship would never work. Gina deserved nothing less than total happiness and a man who would love her. He didn't know how to love, and from experience, he knew he was incapable of learning. He didn't know where to begin.

Gina wanted him to cancel this meeting—he'd even bet her reasons were strictly charitable. But he had to do what he had to do. A long time ago, he'd promised himself he'd never live by others' desires again—unless you counted the air force, and that wasn't what he meant.

As long as he lived, he'd never be able to stand to

love and lose another person. A shame, too, since Gina definitely seemed one-hundred percent woman, and that made her one-hundred percent his type, at least where sex was concerned.

He sighed. So went life.

"What's wrong?" Gina called on her way up his driveway. "I thought you'd be in the car and revving up the motor by now." Before he could answer, her eyes widened and darted wildly from his empty hands to the car to the front porch steps.

"Matt, where's the cake?"

He couldn't tell her the only things he'd been feasting on were the sight of her shoulders and the thought of her naked. So he said, "I ate it."

She raised her eyebrow in disbelief.

"Okay, okay, even you aren't that gullible. Would you believe Frankie ate it?"

"I'll believe it better be in the car," Gina said, charging past him. He'd put it on the passenger seat. She breathed a sigh of relief and turned to him. "It's a good thing we aren't really married. If we were, I'd be chewing you out by now."

"No, you'd be in my bed by now, because if we were married, there would be no way I'd waste our time together trying to convince my father I'm happy."

Her forehead wrinkled for only a second as she tried to decide how to take *that* coming from him. She decided he was only pretending to be a gracious husband. She was proved right when he extended his arm to her.

She raised her eyebrow again in question.

"I thought I'd escort you to your side of the car so we can get used to touching each other," he said.

"I'll just have to grin and suffer through this part, I guess." She tried hard not to think about the way her fingers were resting on the hard muscles of his forearm, how large his hands were, or how strong he seemed. He made her feel petite and delicate, instead of a bit too plump, as Mac had called her from time to time.

Startled, she realized she hadn't thought of her dead husband in a while, that all her thoughts had been filled with the man who was now opening her car door for her. Matt, who made her breathe just a little too fast. Matt, who made her crazy. She was just beginning to understand that he had changed her life from the second she'd slid under the bushes.

And he was leaving tomorrow. He'd told her that.

The breeze blew the scent of roses from her bush around them. Breathing deeply as she got into the car, Gina decided it was an evening for lovers. Watching Matt round the front of the car to get in, she wondered. Should she? Dare she give in to this desire that had begun to permeate every inch of her being? A desire that had absolutely nothing to do with the very thing she lived, breathed and hoped for—love?

As Matt backed the car out, he braked abruptly as the Simmons boys whizzed by on their bikes and kept going. Normally, Gina wouldn't have thought twice about that, but instead of continuing to back out when the street was clear, Matt watched them ride toward the corner, frowning.

"What's wrong?" she asked.

"Not a thing." Turning his head, Matt smiled at

her. She decided to get back to why he'd been watching Frankie later if she remembered. Right now, there was business to take care of.

"Before you pull out—did you remember a ring?"

Matt slapped his palm against the steering wheel and then put the car in park. "I knew there was something—"

"That's what I figured." Balancing the cake on her lap, Gina unzipped her purse and pulled out a small, black-velvet-covered box, which she flipped open with a smirk that said she was pleased with herself. "Some husband you are."

Matt, watching her take the ring from the case, felt suddenly distressed. His hand covered hers, stopping her, and she looked up at him, startled.

"This wasn't from your marriage?" he asked.

A horrified look covered her face. "I wouldn't use Mac's ring!" Her heart thumped painfully at the very thought, and she took a breath, feeling like she was slowly coming to her senses. What in the world was she doing, posing as Matt's wife, making a sham of the institution of marriage and purposely lying to someone? No matter how understandable Matt's reasons, this went against every grain of morality in her body.

"This ring is a sample from my shop. I told you, I consider marriage sacred—and that included the one I had."

"I know you do." Matt reached out and tilted her chin upward. The seconds seemed to tick away as Gina's heart melted at the look in his eyes. It was a look of loneliness, heartache and need all rolled into one.

"I shouldn't be putting you through this," he said. "I know it isn't right of me to ask anyone into my mess. Only if I call tonight off, Gina, I'm afraid I'll never put my past behind me." He hesitated. "Please don't desert me now. I need you."

Matt didn't even know it, but to Gina, he'd uttered the magic words. He needed her. He was hurting, and she'd never been one to put her own needs first. She was strong. She'd survive tonight—as long as she remembered this was only a game for her and Matt. So she wouldn't back out on him now, even though she'd probably be damned in the process.

His hand fell back to the wheel, and he waited.

"You need me just for tonight?" she whispered, wanting to have this absolutely clear in her mind so there were no false hopes later.

"Just for the next hour or so." Hesitating, Matt knew it was important for her to understand the truth about him. "I like you a lot, Gina, but I don't have what you need in me. I'll only make you unhappy if I stay and we try for anything but a one-night stand. I won't risk that."

"Just so we understand each other." She blinked and smiled. What he had said was nothing less than she'd expected, but that still didn't mean she couldn't be disappointed. Somewhere in the back of her mind, she had started to hope.... "But you don't know what you're missing."

Yes, he did, Matt thought. "At least you're mine for the next hour," he said, but his heart wasn't in the grin he gave her. Reaching down, he pushed the ring on her finger. They both stared at their hands for a long minute.

He should have kept searching another couple of days and taken his chances on a stranger, Matt thought. No matter how badly he felt about his father, he was wrong to have dragged Gina into this.

But on the other hand, he could tell Gina cared about him and would do her utmost to make certain his father was left with the impression that he was a happy man. That was what he wanted, no matter what.

So until it was over, he would have to fight his desire for her. The last thing he wanted to do was compound the mistake of using her with another mistake of taking her to bed without having real love for her in his heart. One was bad enough, but he would hate himself for the other.

Gina waved her hand. "Go. The sooner we get there, Matt, the sooner we can leave. Then you can come back here, pack your bags and get out of my neighborhood."

"It isn't big enough for both of us?"

As tense as Gina felt, her lips twitched upward at his quip. She didn't want to laugh. Everything was wrong at that moment. It was wrong that she desired Matt so desperately; it was wrong that he was doing this to his father and to himself; and, finally, it was wrong that lightning never struck twice when it came to love for her.

She couldn't do much about her desire for him, and she couldn't make him fall in love with her. But she had the knowledge, and experience, to do something about his relationship with his father. Somehow, she was going to find a way to help Matt, whether he wanted it or not.

7

Ten minutes into their visit with Luke Gallagher, Gina felt a pang of pity for the man. Matt's father was so eager to please his son. The house was spotless, and Luke had brewed a pot of tea for her and coffee for Matt and even served slices of her lemon cake on paper plates for them. But the harder Luke tried, the more closed off his son became, giving one-syllable answers to Luke's questions and not volunteering anything.

The only thing Gina could say for her "husband" was that he couldn't have been more attentive to her. Matt sat next to her on the couch, his arm resting on the cushions behind her. His fingers kept reaching around and trailing paths along her neck—never lewdly, but that didn't matter. The intimacy of his touch made her insides quiver. She crossed her arms. Matt began to play with her earlobe, and her breath caught. His attention should be on his father, not on playing with her. She needed to do something.

"Do you have any lemon?" she asked Luke to get a few seconds alone with Matt.

As it happened, Luke did. As soon as he left the room, she turned to Matt.

"Please don't touch me like that. You're making me nervous," she whispered.

"Nervous?" he asked. He met her eyes and asked, "Or hot?"

"You should concentrate on your father," she advised.

His eyes shaded over and his face took on an unreadable expression. "I'd prefer to keep my mind on you."

"You're asking for it," she whispered.

"Will I like it when I get it?" he asked.

To her irritation, her mouth twisted of its own accord in suppressed mirth. Before she could think of a suitable retort, Luke was back with a small sandwich plate filled with slices of lemon. Its tangy scent filled the air as he handed it to her.

"Thank you," Gina said, giving Matt's father a sincere smile as she took the plate.

"Pucker power," Matt whispered in her ear.

"Behave yourself," Gina said aloud.

Matt grinned.

Luke frowned at them in confusion, and Gina leaned forward to put a slice of lemon in her tea. "You'll have to forgive your son. He's acting a little frisky this evening. So tell me, Mr. Gallagher, do you like Bedley Hills?" She supposed she ought to worry about eventually running into Luke at some point in the future, but he'd lived in her town for a while now and they hadn't met yet.

"I don't get around much, but it seems like a pleasant town," Luke said. "Of course, when Matt showed up, it knocked me for a loop."

"I must admit, I felt exactly the same way," Gina

said without thinking. Matt's thigh hit hers, and she glanced up at Luke. "Uh, that is, Matt never told me his mother had written him where you were until just recently. I didn't know for a long time what he had planned to do here in Bedley Hills." At least she was telling the truth, Gina thought triumphantly. She thought she heard Matt sigh.

"And you'll be going back to Germany after Matt's leave is up?" Luke asked.

Gina didn't know. She sipped her tea, hoping that Matt would tell Luke what he wanted his father to know, but he didn't say anything. Luke's face fell, and as another minute passed silently, he looked anguished.

Gina jutted out her jaw. This was ridiculous. Putting down her tea, she reached over, put her hand on Matt's thigh high enough so that he would notice, and squeezed gently. Sure enough, his face looked like he'd been jolted by electricity, and he sat straight up. Not surveying to see what else might have registered her touch, she just smiled at him and said, "Your father asked you a question, dear. You aren't asleep, are you?" She squeezed his leg again.

"I'm awake." He reached down and grabbed her wrist, giving her a warning look. "Every inch of me is awake."

She turned to Luke and said with a straight face, "Matt suffers from that condition known as somnambulism—you know, walking in his sleep? Sometimes he's snoozing and no one knows. That's why he never says anything even though his eyes are open. All it takes is a single touch from me to bring his body to attention, though."

"Ain't that the truth," Matt muttered, still frowning. Gina glanced at him, wondering why his comment sounded so very sincere. Maybe he was a better actor than she thought.

Looking grateful for the intervention, Luke was on the verge of laughing, but then he caught Matt's scowl.

"Oh, go ahead and laugh," Gina encouraged. "Matt's learned to live with his condition, although it does get a bit edgy when he's in the cockpit. I keep telling him he'd be safer and better off if he went ahead and trained to be an aircraft mechanic instead of a pilot. He could stay on the ground, and everyone knows that aircraft mechanics are the real strength behind the air force, anyway."

"Gina." There was a definite warning in Matt's voice that said she might just be going too far.

She shook her head, trying her best to look sad. "But Matt insists on maintaining his rank and his pilot's status. Every time he flies there's the chance that he might fall asleep and I'll lose him, but I keep his life insurance paid up, and the military really does have wonderful widow's benefits."

Luke started laughing, and even Matt's lips twisted upward at the edges. "You wait till I get you home, lady," he said in a half growl, but he grinned wider.

"I'm looking forward to it." Leaning over, she kissed his cheek and then patted his knee. "Taking himself too seriously has been Matt's problem since I met him, Luke, but don't worry. I'm working on his attitude problem."

"I think you're probably the best thing that ever happened to Matt," Luke said softly.

"She is."

Matt's unexpected reply was so forceful Gina's heart skipped a beat and she blushed. Then, fearful she was reading too much into his reaction because she wanted to, she turned back to Luke. "Now, you asked Matt where he was going next, right?"

"He?" Luke frowned.

Another slip. Oh, boy. Posing as a wife wasn't as easy as she'd imagined.

"Yes, he. It's a military thing—a mission," she improvised, hoping she was somewhere near what could be considered the truth. For some reason, Matt didn't want to tell his father where he'd be living next, and she didn't know, so she had to do the best she could. "Matt isn't allowed to say where he's going next. But I can tell you I like this area a lot, and until he's back from the upcoming mission, I might stay exactly where I am in Bedley Hills for a little while." She turned to Matt, whose look was unreadable. "Is that all right with you, dear?"

Matt reached over and pulled her close, giving her a long kiss on the lips and kneading his fingertips into her shoulders. Desire melted Gina, and she had to fight to remember where she was, what she was doing, and why.

Clearing his throat, Luke excused himself for a minute. It was exactly what Matt had been waiting for.

"A secret mission?" he whispered. "What the hell are you talking about? If I want him to know where I'm going next, I'll tell him. I didn't ask you to make up stories like that to make Luke feel better. You're just supposed to act like a wife who's in love with me.''

"Pardon me," she said, shivering inside at how abruptly he had dropped his hands away from her. "But you forgot to give me a copy of the script." Her eyes collided with his. "You might have a point to prove, Matt, but Luke is still a human being."

"Just play the sweet wife, would you?"

"Then just play the happy man you're supposed to be."

That, Matt knew, had been the trouble. He'd been sitting there, sullen, because none of this act they were putting on could ever be true. He wasn't happy, and Gina wasn't his wife. He had to get out of there.

Gina sat, stunned, as Matt rose and walked out the front door. Just then, Luke entered the room, saw his son leave and sank down on his chair, burying his face in his hands.

"I'd so hoped that somehow Matt could come to terms with what I did," Luke said, his voice weak. "He isn't happy, is he. Even with you, even with a career he loves, what I did still hounds him."

Guilt surged through Gina at the lie she and Matt had just acted out. She wanted to confess, but Matt might never come to see his father again, and at least Luke would have the small comfort of believing that his son had a good wife who would take care of him. She couldn't take that away from Luke—he had little enough as it was.

Lord, she felt for Matt's father, who seemed only to want his son back, and for Matt, who was unable to deal with the past that still haunted him.

Wanting to do something, Gina rose. Walking over

to Luke, she leaned over and patted his hand. Luke immediately responded by straightening in his chair and regaining his self-control. Reading his body language, Gina saw the older man could deal with this. However weak Luke Gallagher might have been in the past, he had changed.

"Is your life better now, Luke? Under control?"

Luke nodded.

"Then between us, maybe we can help Matt—but only if he wants it badly enough." She had no idea if that were true, since Matt would probably leave town in the morning, but she knew she wanted to try. These two men needed her. "Just please don't give up what you've achieved for yourself because of the way Matt's acting toward you."

Luke nodded again, slowly, thoughtfully. "I won't."

"You have no idea where Matt's brother is?"

"No." A hopeful look crossed his wrinkled features. "I've been looking—but don't tell Matt that."

"I won't."

"If I find West, maybe it will help Matt."

"And then again, maybe it won't," she said softly. West would not be the same person Matt knew years before. The two brothers might not have anything in common except blood ties and bad memories. "Matt needs to heal himself, Luke. No one else can do it for him."

"You're good for him."

"For all the good it does." Tears stung Gina's eyes, and she bit down on her lip to regain her control. "Matt is going away soon, for the military. I can't go with him. I'm hoping that he makes his peace with you, and himself, before he leaves." She glanced at the door. "I'd better get out to the car."

"He's waiting for you, isn't he?" Luke asked, standing and, just like Matt did so often, pushing his hand back through his graying dark hair. "If he isn't, I'll drive you home."

"I'm sure he waited." Gina was positive Matt wouldn't abandon her to walk home alone. He just wasn't that type. Once again, she took Luke's hand and squeezed it gently. "I'll do my best to get him to visit you again."

"Thank you."

Nodding, she headed out the door. Matt *was* sitting in the car waiting for her, and Gina turned to wave at Luke to let him know she'd be okay.

"I'm sorry," Matt said immediately when she joined him. "I guess I blew that, didn't I?"

"Why did you walk out?"

He turned the key in the ignition and half grinned without looking at her. "Somnambulism?"

"I know, I know," she said, waving her hand. "Bad joke. But you laughed." He seemed determined to ignore his feelings about the meeting that had just ended, to keep their current conversation light. Well, she could do that—for now. She watched the lights on the houses as they drove and she thought.

"What I should have told your father when you didn't answer his questions," she said after a while, "was that you learned to nap quickly when you were in prison. You know, it was safer if you hardly ever slept."

Matt shook his head, grinning as he made a right

turn onto their street. "Having you as a wife was more than I anticipated."

"I know I made a couple of slipups, but I think I handled myself well," she said.

Matt didn't answer at first. His face thoughtful, he pulled into his driveway, turned off the headlights and killed the motor. He got out and Gina had no choice but to follow suit. But she didn't want to leave him like this. By the time she got up in the morning, Matt might well have packed and left town, and she would never see him again.

Rounding the car, she faced him, ready to ask him not to go yet, wanting to implore him to straighten out his life. Damning the feelings within her that made her feel for people in trouble, she ignored the inner voice that told her to just walk away.

She couldn't. He needed her too much, and she'd gotten too damned involved to pull away now. If she did, she would feel as though she'd failed somehow. She didn't understand it, but at the moment, that didn't matter. Matt was the important one right now.

"What happened tonight, Matt? Why did you walk out?"

"*You* did a wonderful job, Gina," he said quietly. "I was the one who wasn't convincing, so I left before I said something to him I'd regret later." He reached up and put his hands on her shoulders. "We'll need to pay my father another visit, and this time, I'll have my act together. I promise."

Gina's mouth dropped open. He couldn't really be planning on carrying on his charade after the way he'd acted that evening. "I can't play your wife any longer," she said. "Nothing on earth could convince me to continue to lie to your father."

"Nothing?"

She shook her head resolutely. Explaining the anguish on his father's face when Matt had walked out wouldn't faze the man, so she didn't tell him why she couldn't lie again. Instead she repeated, "Nothing."

"I need you, Gina," he said quietly.

She took a deep breath, and her heart began to pound. "Matt, don't do this," she said, feeling herself weaken.

"I wasn't lying at Luke's house," he said, stepping forward until her back was against the car, and their bodies touched, her breasts pressing against his chest, aching with a sudden surge of need. "You *are* the best thing that ever came into my life."

With a gasp of breath, her mind heady with desire, she stared up at him.

"So what will it be?" he asked, his voice thick.

Her eyelids fluttered as she tried to collect thoughts that were in turmoil. Sighing, she finally was forced to admit the truth.

"Umm, Matt? I think I forgot the question."

"The question was," Matt said thickly, "can I make love to you?"

Even though every inch of Gina felt tight with wanting him, and she felt almost drunk with passion, she had to smile at him. "That wasn't the question."

"I thought you didn't remember it," he said, laughing. He was determined to ignore what had just happened, Gina realized. She'd been wrong. She wasn't the one currently in denial—he was.

But then again, tired of dealing with so many prob-

lems when her desire was overruling her common
sense and her body was literally throbbing with need,
Gina thought denial sounded damned good to her,
too.

"You want to make love?" She tilted her head
from side to side, pretending to ponder the question.
"Out here, where the neighbors can see?"

"I've got nothing to hide," he said.

"Am I speaking to the same man who put up the
Do Not Disturb sign? *You* have nothing to hide?"

"You've seen one body, you've seen them all."

"I'll bet that's not what Babs Tywall would say if
she saw *your* body naked."

He moved his thumb along her chin. "Hmm. What
would she say?"

"I don't know. Why don't you show me what you
have, and then I'll be better able to speculate," she
suggested, lowering her mouth and brushing her lips
across his thumb.

Taking her hand in his, Matt pulled her along with
him until they were inside his screened back porch.
There he gave her a kiss that made her toes curl.

"No lights?" she teased breathlessly. "I thought
you had nothing to hide."

"We wouldn't want Babs to get any sneak pre-
views," he said, catching her hand and kissing it.
"You never did answer my question about making
love."

"Yes, I did," she said softly. "I'm still here."

Leaning down, Matt gave her another slow, long,
hot kiss, his lips devouring hers, filling her with more
heat and desire than she thought a person could ever
have with her clothes still on.

"Let's go inside," she whispered. "I have this sudden inexplicable urge to be naked."

"I think I'm in heaven," Matt said, taking her hand.

He unlocked the back door to the house. Inside, he flipped it shut and hit the dead bolt. She raised an eyebrow.

"Just in case Frankie decides to roam the neighborhood looking for fun."

"Frankie wouldn't do any—"

He pulled her into his arms and began to kiss her, starting at her mouth.

"Such—"

He laid another kiss on her cheek and then moved to the curve of her chin.

"Thing," she finished as Matt's mouth skipped past the neckline of her halter dress to her shoulder.

He moved around her to lick his tongue down the bared skin of her back and then up to her neck. "What were you saying about Frankie?" he murmured.

"Frankie who?" she whispered back as he ever so slowly pulled open the zipper down the back of her dress. She wore a strapless bra, and his fingers unhooked that, too, never once ceasing his kisses on the sensitive part of her neck. Once she was unzipped and unhooked, he slipped his hands under the linen of her dress to cup her breasts.

"I have wanted you since the first time I saw you," he told her, his voice husky in between kisses. "You are so beautiful."

"You don't need to talk, Matt. Just make love to me." Gina didn't want to hear anything false tonight.

Matt's implying to Luke that she was the best thing that had ever happened to him came back to haunt her now. If he had lied, she didn't want to know. During all of her times with Mac, she'd never felt anything with him like what she was feeling now, all this erotic desire, and the fact that love could in no way be involved in frightening her. Gina didn't want to hear Matt say that her body was beautiful, and that he'd never made love to anyone like her. She didn't want to hear him say anything at all, because then she would have to *think* about the truth of what she was doing. If she did that, she would pull away and go home, and she didn't want to.

His thumbs rubbed the rosy peaks of her breasts, and her head fell back against him. She pressed herself against his hardness and moved her hips in a circle in time to his movement, wanting to entice him, wanting to thrill him as much as he was exciting her.

Since his hands were occupied, she unbuttoned the neck of her dress. It dropped down past her waist. Matt pulled it all the way off, revealing her lacy bikini panties.

He groaned as pure pleasure cascaded through him. Hearing the sound, Gina turned and covered his mouth with her own, just in case he was going to make a comment. But speech seemed the last thing on his mind as he slipped his hand down over her most vulnerable place.

His hand was warm and big, and in the panties she was next to naked. As she rode his hand she began to throb inside and finally understood what made men's bodies react with the abrupt suddenness that they did. Chemistry. Pure physical reaction. This was sex at its most basic level.

Sex. Not love. It was all right, Gina told herself. Later, she'd justify this somehow. Right now, she just wanted Matt desperately.

Their mouths locked together, and she bent and began unbuttoning his shirt with an urgency that he was feeling, too. He broke away and helped her with the buttons.

"We're in the kitchen," he pointed out.

Finishing his shirt, she flashed him a wicked smile. "Haven't you heard good sex doesn't depend on where you do it—it's the *how* that counts?"

"Yeah, well, my *how* won't work on a kitchen table," he said, grinning.

"Are you sure about that?" she asked.

"Take my word for it." He wrapped his arms around her. "My how is a lover of luxury and softness," he added, sliding his palms down to cup her buttocks.

Gina wet her bottom lip as he pressed his hardness into her and began to kiss her neck. She had to swallow before she could say, "Your how seems very happy right where it is."

"You have a point," he muttered against her neck. "Oh, Gina, women don't come any softer or sweeter than you."

Gina realized if she did nothing else but bring Matt an hour of true happiness this evening, it might be more than he'd had in a long time. Somehow, she wanted to make his life all right for him again, and if she could do that while assuaging this hunger for him she felt inside her, well, then, a lot of people never got—or gave—even that much.

"I think we'd be a lot more comfortable upstairs," Matt whispered. His mouth sucked on her ear, doing wild, wonderful things to the intensity of her desire for him. For a second, Gina couldn't move, and really didn't care where she was. But then Matt lifted her straight up until her toes no longer touched the floor and, kissing her, half eased her through the doorway into the living room. They made it as far as the sofa, an oversized, overstuffed monstrosity that Mr. Tuttle had supplied for Matt. It was like lying back on a cushioned cloud.

Matt eased off his jeans, and Gina pulled his shirt off. The intensity of her desire made her brush her lips across his nipples. It made her more reckless at lovemaking than she'd ever been in her whole life— and she didn't care.

Naked, supporting his weight on his arms, he slid over her, nuzzling her neck and running his tongue over her now-hot skin. She pushed her breasts up against his rock solid chest, feeling his muscles moving as he rubbed against her softness. For once, Gina didn't think about tomorrow, wasn't planning out every second of her life, wasn't worrying about everyone else. For once she was living for herself, being wildly selfish....

"And loving it!" she whispered as she opened her thighs and lifted her hips, ever so slightly.

"I'm glad to hear that." He slid into her easily, like they'd been built for each other, and then, with great control, he stopped moving and looked into Gina's eyes. They were wide, framed by dark lashes, and seemed to hold the secrets of the universe—the secrets he'd been searching for since he'd first been left alone. He became lost in her smile, and in the sweetness and softness he'd been wanting for so long. It was like he'd finally found what was missing in his life—and he was sad because he knew he'd never be able to hold on to it.

Sensing his distress, Gina lifted her arms and slipped them around his neck, pulling him close and forcing him back into motion. She gave her all to him, and he made love to her as tenderly and unselfishly as he could, cursing himself inwardly because he knew he was only going to end up hurting her.

Gina had never felt so sexual, so free, as she did when finally her body shuddered with the release it had been seeking since...since...since the day she'd first eyed Matt Gallagher. When Matt tumbled over the precipice with her and then rested on top of her, she lay still, her eyes closed, thinking.

She couldn't let Matt disappear from her life yet. But what exactly she expected out of him that he'd be able to give her she didn't know. More sex? If she were willing to settle for that, no matter how wonderful it was with him, she was going against everything she'd ever believed about the sanctity and goodness of love. She didn't want to have changed like that.

But after what had just happened, she was very afraid she already had.

8

Later, as she lay curled in Matt's arms upstairs in his bed, Gina concluded that there was only one way she could keep Matt in Bedley Hills for a while longer.

"You win, Matt," she said softly, running her fingers up his biceps. "I'll pretend to be your wife again."

Matt shifted her until she had to look up at him. "What made you change your mind?"

"The fact that practicing was so much fun?" she quipped, wiggling both eyebrows suggestively. He gave her a wry grin, but the question was still in his eyes. She couldn't answer it. She wasn't ready yet to say anything about her real reason for giving in, not when she had so many doubts in her mind that she could ever make a relationship work with Matt.

Before she'd spoken, Matt had been thinking about his visit with his father. Now that Luke was positive he was unhappy, Matt's inclinations told him to visit again and this time do the job right. Except now he was thinking more of Gina than of himself. Until a second ago, she hadn't wanted to return, hadn't wanted to keep lying. Now she was willing, just for him, just because they had made love.

It wasn't right. Just knowing him was warping her, changing her into someone who would compromise her principles, and Matt couldn't stand to see that happen. He wasn't worth it, because he could never be the man she wanted. So there was only one thing left for him to do.

"I'm calling it off, Gina," he told her, cradling her in his arms. "I've changed my mind about lying to my father."

"So you're going to tell him the truth?" Gina asked, turning over and searching his shaded eyes, a surge of excitement skittering through her. If Matt came to terms with his past, then maybe he could open himself up and become the kind of man who could offer her what she needed—security, commitment and, above all else, love.

"No, I'm going to leave Bedley Hills." He stared down at her, watching her reaction. "Tomorrow."

Gina's excitement that she might have longer to help Matt was abruptly replaced by dismay and disappointment. He was bailing out not only on his father, but on her. She thought that a man who'd changed his life like Matt had ought to have more strength of character than he was showing. But apparently, she was wrong. Matt's way was to walk away from people before he got hurt. She didn't know if she could change him, but she did know that she had to try.

Matt frowned as he watched her face mirror her dismay. He felt bad for her, but it was best he got out now, early, while she still had her heart intact. "I warned you I wasn't good for much."

"Oh, I don't know," she said, letting her fingers walk up his chest and forcing herself to smile, just as she always had when her parents were at their worst. Before she made him face what he was doing, she wanted to soften him up and make sure he realized she was not the enemy. "I thought you were very good for at least—" she glanced at the clock "—the last hour and a half."

His lips curved into a slow grin. Gina thought he even looked relieved she wasn't arguing about his leaving. "I was that good, huh?" he asked. "Hope that rumor doesn't get around. The women will swarm on me like bees on honey."

"Ha! I should have known better than to try to build up a man's ego—it works, and you pay."

"Haven't you ever heard—be careful what you wish for? You might get it?"

"I got it, all right," Gina said, rolling onto her elbow, leaning forward and running her tongue down the side of his neck. She didn't know if he was softening up, but she could honestly say she'd never felt more relaxed in her life.

"If I'm that good, should I get a barbed wire fence to keep the women away?"

She stopped what she was doing and grinned back at him. "Did you ever need it before?"

"To keep women away? Nope. I seem to do that all on my own. But I can honestly say I've related better to you than to any other woman I've ever met."

"That's probably because I'm a sucker for kids and stray animals—"

"I'm not a kid, so I must be an animal, huh? Did you come to that conclusion from the last hour and a half?"

"I was about to add, *and lonely hearts,* but if you want to be an animal, Matt—" flipping onto her back, she flung her arms over her head, exposing her breasts "—then go for it."

Grinning, Matt began another stream of kisses up and down the slopes of her breasts. It wasn't until much later, when he lay resting against her, both of them drifting with the sweet peace of lovemaking, that Gina remembered that he was leaving in the morning. The glorious feeling inside her fled, replaced by an anxiousness she couldn't remember ever feeling. She had to *do* something.

"Have you changed your mind about leaving?" she whispered.

Gina felt his chest heave against hers as he sighed and pushed himself off her. "I'm still going. I can't tangle you up in this mess I've made any further."

"Don't worry about me." Pausing for a second, she added, "If you stay a few more days and resolve this thing with your father, we could play husband and wife until you tell him the truth."

He didn't reply. That was encouraging, Gina thought. If she had that much affect on him, maybe she *could* weaken his resolve. "You need to try again, Matt."

Matt didn't know what to say. He had been looking most of his life for someone who could give him the same feeling of belonging, of stand-by-your-side loyalty that West had, and he'd never found anyone who'd measured up—until Gina. Could he try to change just for her? Did she have the kind of loyalty he needed, the kind of caring he'd been desperately searching for? If he tried a relationship with Gina, would he warm up a little as a human being? Could she teach him to love? Matt felt gut-wrenching, cold fear. He didn't know, and he had to admit he was scared to death to find out and risk disappointment.

How much easier it was to go through life cold and unfeeling. If you didn't get involved emotionally, you didn't suffer. He shouldn't have taken Gina to bed. Now he was thinking of things that could never be.

"I have to be settled in Virginia by the first of the month," he said, still watching her. "If I stay, it'll only be that much worse for both of us when I leave."

"Will it be worse for us if you leave later?" she asked gently. "Or will it be worse for you because you'll be sticking around, lying to your father when you know you aren't happy?"

Matt stiffened inside. It had been so easy to avoid this kind of self-examination in the past, but now Gina's questions were hanging in his mind. His need to make his own decisions fought with his desire to make Gina happy, and he had a feeling she wouldn't be until he proved to her he was doing the right thing with his life.

Rolling off the bed, he reached for his jeans.

"You've been running from your past for a long, long time, Matt," she said, trying to make him talk this out. "Isn't it time you faced it and fought to be happy?"

His fingers rested on the snap of his jeans as he regarded her with his solemn dark eyes. "Have you always been like this, Gina? Reaching out, caring for everyone but yourself?''

''Of course I care for myself.'' She met his gaze stare for stare.

''Then why isn't someone as sweet as you already married with a family of your own? Why are you playing mama bear to all the kids and half the adults in the neighborhood instead of finding some nice guy who will treat you like a princess and give you kids of your own to spoil?''

Her chin jutted out and her eyes filled with tears. He was so obviously telling her that he wasn't the man for her. She'd known that, but still, knowing that there was no hope for them hurt.

Reaching out, Matt brushed his fingers along her neck and the silky ends of her hair. ''Maybe you had to meet me so you'd start trying again to find someone else, I don't know. I do think you're as good as I am at not facing your problems, Gina. Maybe after I leave, you'll choose to stop hiding, too. When you do, you'll see it isn't as easy as you think.'' Abruptly, he reached for his shirt and headed toward the door. ''I'm taking a walk. Stay as long as you like.''

As he walked out the door, Matt knew he shouldn't have said what he did to her. He had no right. Every piece of him felt low-down and guilty for taking things so far with Gina. His only excuse—and it was a pitiful one—was that she was so sweet, so warm and so *good* that he'd been desperate to latch onto everything that she was. He hadn't meant to hurt her. With his past, he never wanted to hurt *anybody*—he knew too well how bad it felt. But he couldn't go back to comfort her, because nothing had changed, and he'd only make her hurt worse.

Damn him, anyway! After Matt left, Gina lay back on the pillows, wiping away tears and feeling like her heart was breaking. Matt was wrong. She wasn't hiding; she *embraced* life, and she never lied to herself.

So why was she crying? Because she'd compromised her principles and had sex with a man she didn't love? She wasn't sure, but she didn't think that was it, if only because she'd never had any expectations about tonight.

A few minutes later, she finally pushed herself out of bed, started dressing and began to figure out the answer. She was upset because, just like with her parents and most of the couples she'd counseled, she hadn't changed a thing for Matt. She'd *failed* him, just like she'd failed the others. And right along with that went her horrible realization that, like everyone else she'd met in life except for Mac, Matt didn't need her.

Now he was determined to leave. Well, let him. Her life would go on. Sure, she liked and admired him. But he was a troubled man, and she didn't need that in her life. She'd just go on as she had—without men—and she'd force herself to be happy. Status quo. Alone and liking it.

She'd be alone. Buttoning her dress, she paused to wipe away fresh tears, and then, suddenly, she sank down on the bed. Alone and liking it? Who was she kidding? Since Mac had died, she hadn't been as involved with anything or anyone as she'd been with Matt. He was the first challenge she'd met with open arms in a long time, and he exhilarated her. Here she was letting him walk right out of her life instead of fighting to really help him and beat her losing streak! The going had gotten rough again, and Matt was right—she was wimping out and retreating.

He might be right, she thought, but she'd be damned if Matt was going to have the last word in this. Slipping into her shoes, she started toward the stairs, fully dressed and absolutely resolute. One more time. She had to try one more time to succeed in helping him. In the process, maybe she would even help herself.

Cursing, Matt paced on his porch early the next morning, unable to leave. He was ready. His suitcases had been in the car since late last night, and his tank was filled. There was only one hitch.

He glanced at the bushes, knowing that somewhere on the other side of them was Gina. When he'd returned from walking, resolute that he had to leave, she had already left his house and gone back to hers. He wanted to say goodbye, but he thought going over there now to do so would only add insult to the injury he'd already caused her.

He paced faster. After she'd left, he'd spent the rest of a sleepless night packing his things, and then tossing and turning in bed, unable to forget her smile. Without her warmth and caring beside him, he'd been left with nothing but the same old cold emptiness he'd had since he'd been a child to keep him company. Only now the cold had evolved from manageably chilly into a killing Arctic front.

He was a damned fool for not pursuing her, but he

was scared. Since his father had walked off, he'd always felt like he was on the outside looking in, and where relationships were concerned, he guessed he'd helped that feeling right along. All his life he had left people behind before they could do it to him, and he'd be left with the pain. How much easier it had been before Gina, when he was still the iceman.

He swore. With his people record, Matt figured marriage or anything else forever—like love—was well out of his reach. But now, he was leaving Gina, and that was proving to be harder than he'd ever believed it could be.

But he had to go. With determination, he bounded off the porch toward his car—and then he stopped in his tracks. His mouth twisted as he stared at his car and figured out why it seemed out of kilter. Someone had let the air out of all his tires, and he had a feeling he knew who.

Frankie. When he got his hands on that kid... Frustrated, he slapped the side of his car, then cursed as his thumb whacked the wrong way on the door handle.

"Damn you, Frankie," he cursed loudly as he shook his hand to get the blood circulating, "I'm going to paddle your vandalistic little a—"

"I hope you were going to say *behind*," Gina called from the sidewalk at the end of the driveway. "There's a town ordinance against public swearing."

Matt stared at her smiling face. Why was she in such a good mood? He forgot that question as he took in the rest of her. She was dressed in terry-cloth-type shorts that hugged her hips, with a sweatband around her head, and a sexy little jogging T-shirt Matt swore she'd worn to make his last minutes in Bedley Hills miserable.

"Get up here," he ordered. "I need to talk to you."

"Well, I don't know, Matt. Is it safe to trespass?" she asked, not moving off the sidewalk. "I was going to wait until you left before I jogged all over your front lawn."

Something was up. Maybe she'd decided it was better if he left, after all. That served him right, but it also hurt.

"Sure, it's safe," he told her. "But you'll have to wait on that jog. I'm going to be stuck here for a while."

"How much longer?" she asked.

"Long enough to find Frankie and give him what for. Messing with a man's car. It ought to be outlawed—"

Like her body ought to be outlawed, he thought, diverted by the sight of Gina's breasts bouncing as she jogged up the driveway toward him with just a little too much gusto.

"What did Frankie allegedly do to you now?" Gina asked in a sweet voice as she jogged in place. Her full breasts jumped right along with her, and Matt gulped as his insides tortured him about his decision to leave the woman behind.

Staring into her eyes as best he could, considering she kept moving, Matt tried to concentrate on the vandalism of his car. But doing so was difficult, as his body tightened in response to her bouncing breasts.

"There's no *alleged* about what Frankie did," he

told her. "You're head of the neighborhood watch, right?"

"Now, you know I am, Matt," she said, doing small lunges to stretch her legs. Matt's eyes returned traitorously to watch her moving her hips and her thighs—

"Do you have to do that in broad daylight?" he growled.

She stretched her arms up in the air, thrusting her breasts outward less than a half an arm's length away from his fingers. "Do what?" she asked, bending over slowly to touch her toes, offering him a view of her cleavage, rounded enough to make his fingers twitch.

"Exercise! Would you just stop?"

"I can't. You aren't supposed to. If your blood stops circulating, it'll pool in your legs and kill you."

"Yeah," he said meaningfully. "That sounds about right, only I'm the one who's going to die here."

Her eyes went wide and innocent. "Matt Gallagher, I am trying to forget that there was anything at all between us, just like you want, and you're accosting me."

"I'm accosting *you?*" he asked indignantly, indicating her outfit with a hard downward glance. "Between that outfit and that body, you're single-handedly making mincemeat out of my concentration. It's almost indecent exposure."

"You didn't think it was so indecent when I was exposed last night," she replied with a smirk.

"No, I guess I didn't do much complaining." His lips spread in a solemn, sheepish smile, and Gina al-

most couldn't bear to keep up the pretense that she
didn't care that he wanted to leave. She took a deep
breath.

"You have a problem with Frankie?" she asked.

"I was vandalized last night," he told her.

Her lips contracted into a pouty grin. "Does that
mean you were a virgin? You should have told me
before we got started—I would have gone a little easier on you."

"Seriously, Gina. I was ripped off."

"What happened, Matt?" she asked. "Did someone steal your privacy?"

Oh, Matt thought, so that's what she was doing. He
understood it now, this one-woman comedy act to
cover either her anger or her hurt over his leaving
town. He felt powerless. He didn't know how to
change himself into the type of man Gina deserved.
He didn't know how to give her the love she needed.

What a mess.

"No," he told her. "Frankie let the air out of my
tires. He stole my freedom."

She stared at him evenly. "I guess that would be
a hanging offense to you, wouldn't it? I'll have to
warn Frankie to keep well away from you."

Matt frowned. She hadn't so much as glanced
down at the tires. Something bothered him about that,
but he wasn't sure what. "I'm certain Frankie did it."

"Oh, really? Did you take a turn at the neighborhood watch last night and catch him in the act? Did
you even bother to ask him about it?"

He shook his head. "No, but—"

"Then you have no proof whatever that Frankie
did it."

"I saw him steal nails out of my shed a few days ago."

She had the good grace to look surprised, and Matt had the bad grace to smirk. "I told you so."

"Oh, now, that I didn't need," she said. With an irritated look at him, Gina started doing aerobic side-stepping, which made him get sidetracked again.

"Would you stop that bobbing around?" he asked. "You don't need to lose any weight, anyway."

Her face softened. "That's always good to hear coming from a man, whether it's the truth or not."

"I never say what I don't mean."

"You just don't talk at all."

He nodded. "I avoid trouble that way."

"You avoid *everything* that way."

Now he *was* getting irritated with her. "So I take it you have no sympathy for this neighbor, just all the rest."

"I'll give you a lift to the gas station so you can blow up your tires. Maybe on the way we can talk about you trying one more time to make a new start with your father. I think you both deserve that."

Boy, now he *was* suspicious. This seemed just a little too pat. Matt studied her eyes. They gazed back at him earnestly.

"I can't forgive him, Gina. I don't believe he won't disappear on me again when I start to care about him."

"You don't know that. You only gave him two short visits to prove himself."

"That was long enough."

Gina's face tightened in anger. "Somewhere along the line, Matt, probably in order to survive, you developed a cynicism that is going to be the ruin of you. The way you see the worst in everyone was self-preservation when you were a kid and no one else was there to protect and comfort you. But now you're an adult. It's time you grew up and started letting yourself trust in the good in people.''

"I grew up when I was eleven years old," Matt said evenly. "Since then, I can count on one hand the people I've trusted—or respected. My father isn't one of them.''

"You are so damned stubborn!" Gina said, her voice rising along with her emotions. "I'm glad you didn't try with me. I'd only end up doing something that would inadvertently blow the whistle on you, and *poof!*" She smacked her hands together for emphasis. "You'd be judge and jury, and then you'd be out of my life again!''

She turned and started walking away, but Matt caught her by the arm and spun her around. "I don't know, Gina," he said tightly. "Suppose you tell me one thing you could possibly do wrong where I'm concerned?''

"Care about you," she said, staring up into his expressionless eyes. "That was enough, wasn't it?''

"I'm leaving because I'd be no good for you," he told her. His voice was even and controlled. "I'm doing you a favor.''

"Bull. You're leaving, Matt, because you won't admit that you need anyone in your life badly enough to trust them." She shook her head, staring down to where his fingers gripped her upper arm—hanging on for dear life, and he didn't even realize it. She raised her eyebrow at him, and he let go of her. Still frowning, she continued, "I forgot that only you can change yourself. I was wrong to try to make you stay one last time."

His mouth dropped open as what she was saying registered. "You let the air out of my tires? You? Miss Do-gooder?"

She blinked at him. "Yeah, me. Every saint has some sinner in them. Before I realized you're happiest being all by yourself, I wanted you to stick around and reconsider reconciling with your father. So what are you going to do now, Matt? Paddle my vandalistic little behind?"

"Now, there's a thought," Matt said between clenched teeth, before letting his breath whoosh out of him. "But instead, I'm just going to get my tires fixed." He nodded when she frowned in disbelief. "Yeah, that's exactly what I'm going to do."

"And *then* you'll leave," she said, shaking her head, sounding really disappointed. "You don't have the character I thought you did."

"If you weren't in love with the idea of being in love, Gina, you could have saved yourself a whole lot of grief by realizing that no matter how much you try to help, I can't change into the kind of man you need. But no, you have to get involved and try to help everyone, don't you. Even when you end up being the one hurt."

He suddenly saw golden sparks of fury and pain in her brown eyes, and she whirled around and half ran down the driveway. Matt swore under his breath. He shouldn't have said that to her. She could no more change the way she was than he could. But her remark about his character had cut him to the bone, and his immediate reaction had been to strike out.

Suddenly he found himself full of an emotion—anger. He did have character, he told Gina silently. Even after being labeled a juvenile delinquent, he'd made something of himself in spite of what everyone thought. He *could* put his life in some sort of order—and he would be happy. And before he left, somehow he'd make damned sure Gina learned just how wrong she was about him.

But first he had to fix his tires.

As it turned out, Eli Tuttle, two blocks away, was only too glad to help, but once again, Matt paid. Not in money this time, but in listening to Tuttle's cackling laughter when he learned what Gina had done to keep Matt from leaving.

"If a woman tried that hard to cook my goose, boy," Tuttle told him, "I'd sure as heck stick around and let her enjoy the meal."

Matt was still too annoyed at Gina to grin. But the old man had a point.

"If you change your mind about leaving," Tuttle added, "just give me a call. You're paid up for a whole month, so it won't be a problem."

That's what Tuttle thought. Maybe his staying wouldn't be a problem for his landlord, Matt thought, but so far, being in this town had been one continuous problem for him.

By the time they'd fixed the flats and Tuttle drove off in his truck, Matt had done a lot of serious thinking about his problem and come to a decision. He was going to try a true reconciliation with his father. Forgiveness just didn't seem to be in him, but at the very least, he figured he could leave his father with good feelings between them. He'd prefer to run, but damn it, he could not leave Bedley Hills until he earned Gina's respect. Why he cared so much what her opinion was of him, he didn't know, but he did.

And maybe, in the meantime, he might get to hold Gina in his arms one more time before he gave her up forever. Even if he believed he could love—which he didn't—he *had* to go to Virginia, and he couldn't see the mama bear of this Bedley Hills neighborhood giving up everything she had here.

Not for the likes of him.

Confident in his decision, he sighed. If he were staying, he'd have to tell Tuttle he'd changed his mind about leaving and then he'd have to go see Gina, beg her forgiveness and ask for her help. With the reaction she was bound to have after what had happened between them, he'd rather get shot down over enemy territory—it would probably be safer.

What, Luke wondered for the hundredth time since Matt had walked out the night before, could he have done or said to make his son believe he'd changed? Probably nothing, his contact from AA had told him, if his son didn't want to reconcile. He'd hurt Matt so badly, there might be no fixing it.

Done with his shift where he worked, needing to divert himself from the heavy sadness inside him, Luke turned on the television to his favorite talk-show hostess. The woman had recently started having very upbeat guests instead of the whining humanity who appeared on most of the other channels. Motivational shows, they were called, and Luke fully enjoyed watching others who had changed their lives for the better.

He settled in with a cup of coffee and listened. Ten minutes later the coffee had been forgotten, and he was riveted to the program, hoping that they would give the phone number for more information over again so he could write it down. The show spotlighted people who had pursued their dreams and achieved them. One woman mentioned a seminar that had helped her given by a man named West or Wes Gallagher—he hadn't been able to tell. Could it be his other son?

For long minutes, Luke waited and prayed that the successful seminar leader so admired by the people on the show was indeed West, and that he would be able to contact him. And most of all, that West hadn't grown so bitter over the years that he didn't want to be reunited with his family. If that were the case, contacting West would be painful, but Luke was desperate enough to help Matt that it was worth a try.

9

After work, Gina plopped down in the most comfortable chair she had in her house and slipped off
her sandals. She'd made it through the day at the
shop, even though, after what Matt had said to her,
her heart didn't seem to be in the hearts-and-flowers
business like it usually was. Every couple who
walked through the door of the shop reminded her of
what could never be between Matt and her.

He was wrong, she insisted silently. She *could* help
him deal with his past. He was just too bullheaded to
want any changes, and that was going to doom him
to spending the rest of his life alone. Well, that was
his choice.

A tentative knock at her door broke into her
thoughts. Right after she'd arrived home, she'd told
Jimmy Simmons she wanted to see Frankie as soon
as possible, planning to ask him about the nails that
he'd supposedly taken. Not that she doubted Matt.
But mistakes could be made, and she wanted the
whole story before she went to Karen, the boy's
mother.

Since she was expecting Frankie, the last person
she expected to see holding a heart-shaped candy box

was Mr. Do Not Disturb himself. Surprise, trepidation and pure joy that Matt was still around kept her from saying a word. What on earth was he up to? She didn't know. But she was still angry about this morning, so she did the first thing that came to her.

She slammed the door shut in his face.

The second knock came a few seconds later, and she yanked it open immediately. "Matt, you are a fool—"

"I know."

Her gaze dropped, and her heart gave a strange little tug as she realized he was down on the concrete on a bent knee. Men like Matt never went down on one knee, unless...

"I came to bring you a peace offering and to ask you a favor," he said.

Gina took a short, quick breath as she took the box he handed her and set it on a small table next to the door. Of course he wasn't proposing. That would be stupid for both of them. Even she knew better. They might have a stormy bond, but she wasn't going to get struck by lightning twice.

"You look uncomfortable," she said, crossing her arms over her chest. "That concrete must be murder on the knees."

"It is. Can I get up now?" he asked hopefully, his dark eyes meeting hers.

"No." She shook her head. His face fell like a little boy's, and her heart went out to him, but still... "Some suffering will be good for your character."

"Good for my character—or for your female pride?"

She gave him a smug smile that held none of her

usual openness. "Look at it this way—if the favor you want is something I don't like, and I hit you over the head, you won't have as far to fall to the ground."

He didn't look at all worried. "Do your neighbors know you have a sadistic streak?"

"It's the first time it's surfaced." Crossing her arms, she added, "You apparently bring out the worst in me."

"I told you that. You just wouldn't listen." He shifted uncomfortably.

"So I'm listening now," she said, stepping out onto the patio. "What's the favor?"

"I wouldn't ask you…that is, I know I shouldn't ask you after the argument we just had…but the fact is that I really care about your opinion of me—"

"Just *ask*, Matt," she said. "And for goodness sake, go ahead and get up."

He did, brushing off his knees and looking relieved. Gina didn't know what to think. He cared about what she thought of him. That had to mean something. But then again, she didn't dare hope that it did. Maybe Matt had the right idea—sometimes it *was* easier not to care about people. Good Lord, she was tired of getting hurt.

"I want you to pose as my wife tonight."

"Since you're too smart to ask me to bed at this point—" she pulled in a deep breath and looked straight at him "—I take it you want to try again with your father?"

He nodded. "I don't know if I can tell him the truth about you, but I can at least get to know him a little better than I do now."

"Why did you change your mind?" If he wanted

only to make Luke miserable, she didn't want any part of it.

"I figured if you went through the trouble of flattening my tires to get me to stay, maybe you had a good reason, and it wasn't that you were worried about my father." His face was earnest, and his eyes examined hers to get her reaction. "You did it to prove something to me, so I thought long and hard and decided I should rethink what I'm doing here. Even if I don't have any feelings for Luke, I can't leave our relationship like this."

She simply stared at him.

"What are you thinking?" he asked, sounding anxious.

"I'm thinking that if counseling is as easy as flattening a client's tires, then I wasted one heck of a lot of time and money on schooling." She wanted to laugh, but somehow, nothing was funny anymore. "Are you still going to let him think you're happy?"

"I'm not unhappy, Gina." His big shoulders shrugged underneath his blazer. "Will you do it? I know I have no right to ask you, but it's just for one more evening."

"After all your talk about my interfering?"

"You're not interfering if I'm asking."

In a warped way, Gina guessed that made sense. She was thrilled he had changed his mind and seemed earnest about making his father feel better, but she was also cynical because Matt still wanted to pretend he was happy, and therefore he wasn't going to be honest. In a way, he was still hiding, even though at least now he was showing he cared.

And last, deep inside her, even though she expected

nothing from him, she was hurt. His change of mind about leaving had nothing to do with *them.*

But despite all that, Gina nodded. This was almost, in a way, what she had flattened Matt's tires to achieve. Father and son would get back together one more time. She could put up with the pretense of being Matt's wife for a little while longer, she guessed, if it brought about the result she wanted—Matt's happiness. If it didn't, at least it would buy her the time and closeness to Matt she needed to try to show him how he could make himself happy.

And if he had to leave her, then she *had* to change the man's life. She couldn't let him go otherwise, knowing he was going to spend the rest of his life alone. She couldn't, because she thought she might be falling in love with him.

Because Matt's father had an AA meeting that night, they had to wait a whole day to visit. Luke offered to skip it, but Matt quickly said they could come the next evening instead after Luke got off work. The last thing he wanted, Matt told Gina, was to be responsible if his father fell off the wagon. To Gina, that sounded promising, as if Matt really might reconsider about his father.

The hour or so they spent at Luke's went smoothly. Matt listened to his father's story of how he'd sunk to the bottom and finally decided he was going to turn his life around. Not going into a lot of detail, Matt even opened up some about his own life, and about how he'd lived on the streets for a while. Luke had listened with tears in his eyes and apologized again for having made him go through that, and Matt simply nodded. Even without the actual words of forgiveness, the atmosphere was peaceful, and Gina sensed the two were beginning to connect.

The only difficult part about the whole time they spent with Luke was that Matt was once again playing the attentive husband. And irritated as she still was with Matt, Gina couldn't keep herself from leaning intimately against the side of him, or resting her hand on his thigh as he talked. Her body seemed to be saying that one night with Matt wouldn't be enough to keep her satisfied forever.

She told her body to shut up.

Too soon, the three of them were walking toward the front door, saying goodbye. Matt was promising to write and telling Luke he had just received new orders that would put them at Langley Air Force Base in Virginia next, instead of where he had been going.

"So Gina can go with you?" Luke asked.

Gina shifted uncomfortably as Matt nodded. Then she watched, her breath catching, as Luke extended his hand to his son. Matt glanced down at it, and a second later, the two were shaking hands.

"I shouldn't have doubted you, Matt," Luke said. "I can see that you've built yourself a nice life. How you managed, I don't know, but I'm happy for you, and I'm proud of you. I can rest easier at night now, knowing that you rose above what I did to you and West and your mom and made something wonderful for yourself."

Gina felt her throat tighten. Matt looked so reserved—couldn't Luke see that? Luke looked so happy, because he believed a lie. It wasn't right. She worked her bottom lip against her teeth, trying to decide what to do.

"I'll be all right, Luke," Matt said, his words sounding heartfelt. "I really will."

"Good. It's been my dream since I sobered up to get everyone reunited if I could." He opened his mouth as if to say something else, then closed it and pumped his son's hand harder.

Gina could feel the seconds ticking away. If she didn't do something now, while the two men were together and could still talk, Matt would leave for Virginia, and it would be too late. He had told her he planned to write his father, but he doubted he would ever come back to Bedley Hills. Seeing his father brought back too many memories, and there was still the fact that his brother was gone. From what he had said to her, Gina was fully aware nothing had really been accomplished tonight for Matt.

Gina blinked and swallowed. Matt wouldn't be able to feel love until someone showed him what love was. She knew what she had to do, and she was fully aware that Matt wouldn't understand it as the loving gesture it was. He would hate her forever.

"You and Gina will keep in touch—I'm counting on it," Luke was saying.

Gina took a deep breath. "Don't worry, Luke, I will, since I live here in town, anyway."

Luke frowned.

"Gina, don't do this," Matt warned softly.

She looked at Luke, because if she looked at Matt, she knew she would see the betrayal he felt in his eyes, and she couldn't bear to see that right now. "We aren't married, Luke. Matt met me a couple weeks ago right here in Bedley Hills and convinced me to pose as his wife so you would think he's having a wonderful life. But he isn't. He's miserable." Her eyes filled with tears. "But he needs somebody in his life, Luke, and if it can't be me, I hope it can be you."

Turning, she fled out the door and to the sidewalk, ignoring the fact that Matt was calling her name, walking away from Luke and Matt as fast as her high heels would carry her. It was still early evening, and light outside, so she hoped Matt would let her walk the mile or so home while he talked things out with his father.

All the way home she fought back the tears, but she thought what she'd done was probably all for the best. Either Matt would put his past to rest and go on with his life, or he'd get his anger out with his father. Either way, he would at least have a chance at happiness. She was certain he wouldn't want her now, but maybe she was probably better off, too. As he was now, they were too different. She frightened him, because she needed to be close. Matt needed his emotional privacy and his physical distance, and she hated that. If dealing with his father helped him, and he came to her, so be it. But she'd dealt with enough people to know she shouldn't hold her breath waiting.

When Gina didn't answer his call, Matt turned back from Luke's door and slammed it shut. Damn that woman. From the second he'd met her she'd played havoc with his life, turned it upside down, kept him so he didn't know if he were coming or going. She had no right to tell Luke the truth. No right at all.

Luke. Blinking, he looked at his father and saw a

man who suddenly looked much older than his sixty years.

"Is it true?" Luke asked.

Matt waited, only his father didn't say anything else. Nothing. The man just stood there, looking like he'd been socked in the gut.

This shouldn't have happened, he thought. He had come here a second time so when he left Bedley Hills, his father would be at peace with his life. Gina had wrecked everything. Never trust anyone, his sense of protection reminded him. How quickly he'd forgotten. The old coldness and caution flooded back into Matt, freezing that warm feeling he'd had inside a few minutes before Gina had dropped her bombshell. A flight of fancy he'd indulged in, thinking Gina was one in a million. Nice while it lasted, but so stupid. Life was for the cynical, not the naive. If you trusted, you got hurt. It was as simple as that.

What Matt couldn't figure out was why Gina had interfered. Revenge? But he guessed the reason didn't matter. It tore him apart that Gina, just like the rest of the people in his life, had looked after her own desires first. She'd wanted Luke to know, so she'd told him, never mind if it hurt or bothered *him*.

"Son?"

"I lied," Matt agreed, facing his father. "Gina told you the truth. I probably am the most miserable human being she's ever seen, only I think she probably meant miserable as in lousy worm."

Luke's eyes narrowed. "You haven't known Gina that long, and she seemed awfully worried about you."

"Gina's made it her life's work to worry about

everyone except herself. She'd be a lot better off if she devoted her energy to finding a good man to fall in love with.'' Matt didn't even want to think about *that* happening.

Luke moved over and sat back down in his chair. "Seems to me there's a lot more going on between you two than what I've heard.''

"And there's going to be a lot more,'' Matt said, pacing the length of Luke's rug. After he was done talking to his father, he was heading to Gina's and he was going to—

Oh, yeah, he thought, halting his steps suddenly. She was female, so he couldn't deck her.

Suddenly all the fight drained out of him, and he plopped onto the couch, purposely working on relaxing his muscles and his anger. He could yell, though. Right now he thought he could yell at Gina Delaney a whole lot.

But wasn't she at least right about his needing family? Reaching up, he raked his fingers through his hair, and stared at his father, who seemed to be occupied with his own thoughts. He could admit that he'd been just coasting along, alone, and maybe start changing his life for the better, or he could tell his father, See you, and retreat back into his shell. Only, since Gina had come into his life, he'd discovered that his shell was a cold, lonely place, and he'd turned into the crab of the century. He didn't want his life to be like that anymore. He wanted happiness—that much he was sure of.

Deciding that making the right choice didn't mean he had to forgive Gina, he nodded at his father. "She shouldn't have opened her mouth to you, but, yeah, what she said was true. I lied to you about being happy. I do like flying, but apart from that..." He took a deep breath and blurted it out, "Apart from flying and searching for West, I don't really have much of a life." He'd only started to get one when he'd come to Bedley Hills and become Gina Delaney's neighbor.

His father nodded slowly. "I'm sorry. I'll repeat that until the day I die if you need me to. And please know, I'm here if I can do anything for you at all."

Matt nodded, gulping as a surge of heat warmed his face and his eyes. He blinked furiously, and forced his jaw out, stifling down the emotion in his heart. He was acting like a damned little kid. He was a man, and he could handle this. He could handle having family again—at his own pace. Gina shouldn't have interfered.

"Son?"

"I need to think awhile." Matt stood, as did his father. "I do have to leave Bedley Hills for Virginia—I wasn't lying about that. But I might be able to keep some leave days open and get around to see you sometimes."

His father brushed at something in his eye before offering his son his hand. Matt stared down at it for a few seconds, and then he did something he would never have envisioned himself doing before he'd come here.

He leaned forward and hugged his father.

"You're so quiet, I know something's up," Chantie said to Gina as she finished closing out the cash drawer late the next afternoon. "It's that Matt, isn't it?"

"Hmm." Gina slid the drawer in place and locked it. She'd peeked into the driveway next door that morning, and his car was still there, but she had a feeling he'd be leaving soon. Men like Matt didn't change. He hadn't come over to yell at her last night, and she had a feeling that was probably because he was too angry. She'd never hear from him again, and it was her own fault for trying to help him. For once, she should have minded her own business. Matt had warned her....

She had to admit, though, Matt wasn't in first place for the most miserable human being she'd ever run across any longer—she was.

"What I know is that you want him," Chantie said. "What I don't know is why you aren't trying to fight for him."

"Because Matt doesn't want or need anyone, Chantie," Gina replied, locking up the money bag in her small safe. "He worships his privacy, and he doesn't have any friends. Does that sound like someone I could fall in love with?"

"Let me see," Chantie said, resting her elbow on the counter and her chin in her hand. "This guy is a pilot, he's drop-dead gorgeous, and he really likes you. That's as rare as Halley's Comet. If you don't go for it, I'm going to have you declared certifiably insane."

"I've already had *it*," Gina muttered under her breath.

"Whoa, ho, I heard that!" Chantie said, and then asked in a low girl-talk voice, "So how was it?"

"I meant," Gina said sternly, "that the man is making me insane."

"Yeah, sure that's what you meant." Chantie grinned. "A pilot, handsome as sin, he likes you, and *he's good in the sack.* I think I want you to buy me a lottery ticket—you're the luckiest girl in Ohio. You know I'll take care of your store for you. You could follow him to the ends of the earth, and have a happy-ever-after—or two. So what's stopping you?"

"I think you're overstating the simplicity of the situation." Gina walked over to the box of chocolates Matt had used to bribe her. Taking a piece, she offered the box to Chantie, who shook her head. "A relationship between two people should never be based on liking each other and being good in the sack. It can't last. There has to be *love.*"

"Says you. You're spouting that counselor stuff at me while you're eating comfort food," Chantie pointed out. "You'd better take off your white coat and live a little, girl, before you let the best thing that ever happened to you get totally away. Geez! If you don't want him, then at least tell me I can take a stab at him myself."

A wave of jealousy rolled over Gina and her mouth fell open. The word *no* was on the tip of her tongue, but then she remembered—she really didn't have any right to deny Chantie something she didn't hold any claim to.

"Ha!" Chantie pointed her finger at Gina. "Got-cha! If you could have seen how *rocked* you looked when I said that, you'd realize what a deep thing you have for this guy. Maybe you are in love with him, and you don't even know it."

"I'm not in love," Gina denied flatly, popping another chocolate into her mouth and letting the soothing smoothness melt over her tongue. The intensity of the jealousy she'd felt at the very suggestion of Chantie dating Matt was only physical. It had to be. She and Matt weren't in love.

Were they? They couldn't be. Love wasn't a jumble of confusion and wrangled nerves. Love was stable, solid, trusting and dependable. Love was what she'd had with Mac; what she'd sworn would never strike twice.

Wasn't it? She put the box down on the counter.

"That's more like it." Chantie nodded in approval. "You got to keep in shape if you're going to catch a hunk like Gallagher."

Gina shook her head. "He said my body is beautiful."

Chantie moaned. "I should have a man who worships me like this. You say he doesn't know he's in love, either?"

"I am not in love," Gina insisted.

"You aren't in love and you don't want him to stay—"

"Of course I do. I wouldn't have let the air out of his tires if I didn't."

Chantie hooted in glee.

"Oh, Lord, why did I tell her that?" Gina asked, gazing up toward the ceiling.

Chantie laughed harder. "Eating chocolate is mellowing out your brain. Have yourself a couple more pieces and tell me exactly why you messed with the man's wheels."

"It's not for the reason you're thinking. He had

some unfinished business with his father here, and he was all set to run out on it.''

"Unfinished business with you, more like it,'' Chantie said. "When are you going to admit you love him?''

"When?'' Gina echoed. Why hadn't she gone home a half hour ago, so she wouldn't have to deal with these questions?

Because if he hadn't left yet, going home meant Matt would be only yards away from her instead of a mile or two. *Face reality, Gina,* she told herself. *Matt is really light-years out of your reach.*

"When?'' Chantie repeated.

Gina picked up her purse and strung it over her shoulder, killed another minute searching for her car keys and turned to Chantie. "Do you want an answer, or do you want a paycheck?''

Chantie looked nonplussed. "You better figure it out, girl, before you lose the best thing that ever came into your life.''

"Mac was the best thing,'' she denied.

"Mac might have made your eyes twinkle, but every time you talk about Matt, I see something special happening to you.''

"Pray tell, what is that?''

"Flushed cheeks, wide eyes, weak knees and a thoroughly dazed look. Mama called it the love *fever.*''

"It's obvious your mother should have been the relationship counselor, not I.'' Gina turned around and headed for the front door.

"Where are you going?'' Chantie called.

"Home,'' Gina said over her shoulder. "If I do

have this love fever over Matt, about the only thing I can do about it is go home, put my feet up, take a couple of aspirins and hope like all get out that it goes away.''

That's what she hoped, but when she arrived home and saw Matt's car was still in his driveway, she knew there wouldn't be enough aspirin in the world to cure what it was she had.

10

The clock chimed in the hallway, earning a sardonic look from Matt as he stared up at it, and then down at his still-unpacked suitcase. ''Six o'clock, and all is...miserable?''

Miserable was the only word that came close to describing how Matt felt. Now that his father and he had reached a better understanding about things, he ought to be on the road to Virginia. Only, he couldn't bring himself to leave. He was furious with Gina, but on the other hand, he had learned something from being forced to face his father. Something inside him was rebelling at leaving things as they stood with Gina. Was he thawing out? Feeling love? He didn't know. It had been too damned long. How the hell was he supposed to tell?

He took a deep breath. He'd been sitting in this same chair for what seemed like hours, knowing that if he stayed long enough, Gina would get home from her shop and be available if he wanted to go over there and confront her. But he couldn't seem to work up the courage. He was trained to take care of the enemy, for God's sake. How could one little slip of a woman be so threatening to him?

Downstairs, someone knocked on the door. Matt hurried down the stairs, hoping it might be Gina and that somehow, someway, she might have his answer.

I'll never learn, Gina told herself, standing outside by her bushes with her hedge clippers, pretending an interest in her landscaping she didn't have at the moment. Knowing Matt's car was in the driveway, she'd been too restless to stay inside. When he left for good, the masochistic side of her wanted to see him drive away.

So she'd changed into shorts and a T-shirt, picked up her hedge clippers and started trimming bushes that were becoming nubs by now, so she'd be aware when Matt came outside. When she heard what might be a knock on his door, she tried to see through the bushes, but all she got was a face full of small leaves.

Backing away, she willed herself not to stoop so low as to look through the hole for a better view. She was *obsessed.* Had she been one of her own clients in her counseling days, she'd have referred herself to a psychiatrist by now. Even knowing this, though, her feet refused to carry her back inside her own house. Neither could they take her next door so she could beg Matt to be in love with her. If he didn't have it in him, he didn't. Some things she'd finally learned she had absolutely no control over.

A door slammed next door, and she heard Matt's voice ask someone what they were up to. She couldn't help herself. One last look at Matt, and that would be it forever. Hoping she didn't look too obvious if someone noticed her from the street, she bent upside down and peered through the hole. Matt's face was unreadable, but he was hurrying down the steps of his side porch.

"Wait a minute, Frankie, I want to talk to you!" he yelled.

Gina got the overwhelming sense of being thrown into the past, with everything in the same setup as it had been when she'd first met Matt. Excitement rushing through her veins, she caught her breath. Was this her chance to start all over again with him? Almost as quickly, she sobered. If it were, would she do one blasted thing differently?

With the flash of a lightning bolt, she knew she would, and she knew what that thing was, too. Watching as Matt turned and ran down his drive, yelling again for Frankie to stop, Gina sprang into action. If he was going to be mad at someone, it should be at her.

Slipping through the hole, she came up in Matt's yard just as he reached the sidewalk at the far side of his property. She thought he would turn and come back because Frankie had obviously gotten away, but he yelled Frankie's name again and started running down the street.

Boy, she'd really done it—driven Matt over the edge into madness—chasing a kid down the street for nothing! Since there wasn't time to get Frankie's mother, Gina ran after the two of them, wondering how on earth she had let herself sink this far.... She, Gina Delaney, was actually chasing a man, one she swore she had no feelings for. Chantie was going to die laughing.

Elijah Tuttle was kneeling in his front yard when

Frankie whizzed by on his bicycle, barely missing knocking over one of the potted flowers he was transplanting along the front sidewalk.

"Danged kids," he muttered under his breath.

Seconds later Matt ran past him, too, shocking Tuttle so much he lost his balance and fell onto his backside. Staring at Matt's figure as he continued to run, Tuttle added, "Danged kids."

Gina Delaney was the third one to run past, but she noticed him half-sprawled on the grass and stopped. Her face flushed, she panted heavily, then managed to say, "I saw that. Are you all right?"

"Yeah, yeah," he muttered, waving her on. Gina nodded and took off again down the sidewalk in a big hurry. He had just started to pick himself up when Jeb Tywall also strode past, intently staring far down the street in front of him.

"Jeb! What's goin' on?"

"Aim to find out. Can't stop, or I might lose 'em," Jeb told him over his shoulder. "Watcha doin' on the ground? C'mon with me," he urged. "This might be real interestin'."

Tuttle rose to his feet. Frankie on a bike was usual. Matt Gallagher running after him would make for an afternoon of good gossip with the neighbors. But Jeb was right—that sweet Gina chasing after Gallagher was something to look into.

Picking up his cane, Tuttle left his flowerpots and started down the street in their direction.

As Frankie headed deeper into the woods, Matt swore with what little breath he had left over from running three blocks. The kid had started this by knocking on his door and then darting away, and this time, Matt was determined to find out what Frankie was really up to. It wasn't something he *had* to know, of course. It was more like something he had to prove to himself—that he was right about the way he thought about things, about Frankie, and about his life. He wasn't that harsh and unfeeling, it was just that the world really was rotten and he was just taking care of himself.

On the far side of a tree, the boy scrambled off his bike and within seconds disappeared up into the lower depths of the branches. Stopping where he was a few feet away, Matt scowled when he saw where the kid was hiding.

A tree house. Well, that explained why Frankie had taken his nails. Striding closer, he stopped when he saw the cardboard sign nailed into the side of the tree.

He rounded to where he could read it, and when he did, for the second time in two days, he felt like someone had kicked him in the gut. It was his sign that he'd left by his screened-in porch, with some words scratched out and some words squeezed in wherever they would fit—but Matt got the picture clearly enough, misspellings and all.

Mr. Galager's Tree House.
DO NOT DISTURB!
Yes, this means you!

"Frankie," he called upward, watching the leaves shake as Frankie moved around up on the boarded floor, "I'm not certain I understand this."

Silence. And then the boy called down, "My

brother and I made this fort for you, so you'd have some place private to go away from Miss Delaney."

Close enough now to see what was going on, and to hear what Frankie said from the tree, Gina stayed where she was out of sight and listened. As far as she could tell, Matt didn't know he had an audience.

Par for the course, she thought with a small grin.

Matt half smiled upward at where Frankie was hidden behind the walls of his "fort." "You thought I wanted my privacy from Gina?"

"She's a *girl*, isn't she? And she's always spying on you—I've seen her."

That was the last time she made cookies for that kid! Gina thought, almost blurting it out loud. But Matt was grinning up at the tree, and something about this scene taking place in front of her felt so good she couldn't interrupt. Matt needed this in his life. He needed lots of people who cared—before he left to be alone again.

"We just finished the fort today," Frankie was saying. "So I came over to tell you, but you looked mad and you *yelled* before I said one word."

Matt sucked in his breath. There must have been something in his expression that frightened the kid when he'd opened the door at his house. Frankie sounded really upset. "I am so sorry, Frankie. Can I come up and see it?"

"Are you going to hit me?"

"No," Matt promised forcefully, and then his face fell. Did the kids in the neighborhood think he was *that* bad?

Gina could have hugged Matt—Frankie, too. Matt

actually seemed worried about what the kids thought of him.

"Okay, c'mon up," Frankie called. "Mr. Tuttle said you'd be leaving town soon, so I guess it's your last chance, anyway."

His last chance—at finding some kind of inner peace here, in Bedley Hills?

"Frankie, you don't know just how true that is," Matt said. Reaching up, he climbed the ladder, caught onto a thick branch and shifted himself into the fort. He carefully tested the floor, which, thankfully, appeared sturdy enough. Sitting, he glanced at the job the Simmons boys had done.

"Nice," he told Frankie. "My brother and I couldn't have done better at your age." He said this with a smile, because he doubted he and West would have thought to put up the refrigerator-box-size pieces of thick cardboard as privacy walls.

"We decorated it for you," Frankie pointed out. In the corners were two spider plant seedlings and a couple of other items that had turned up missing in the neighborhood. Above Frankie's head, three painted model airplanes swung from strings in the evening breeze. One was an F-15, just like he flew. Matt's throat choked up, and then he saw, thumbtacked into one of the walls, the picture of him with his plane Frankie had taken along with the nails—and Matt's heart. His eyes narrowed and watered, and he brushed at them impatiently. Allergies. Not tears, he told himself. But he knew better.

"Your own private place," Frankie added, still in the far corner, his face wary when he saw Matt's expression. "Don't you like it?"

"Yeah, Frankie. I like this place *a lot*. Where'd you get the wood?"

"Dad. I've been borrowing everything else to make it nice for you."

Matt shook his head, feeling so old, and so wise— yet at the same time, stupid. "Frankie, that's not borrowing. That's stealing." He didn't bother to add that he had done the same thing more than a couple of times to survive on the streets. "And stealing is very wrong, no matter how good the intention behind it."

"No, it isn't stealing," Frankie denied, shaking his head. "We were only keeping the things until you left town, and then we were going to return everything 'cause we're just boys, and we don't need plants and stuff."

Matt had to swallow, and he couldn't talk at first, which was all right, because he didn't want to argue the point about the vandalism. If Frankie was a genius, he was certain the boy would give it some thought. "So you thought I needed a place to hide from Gina?"

Frankie nodded solemnly. "She's nice and all that, but she's lonely for a husband, and you know how desperate lonely widows can be."

"Ha!" Gina said from below the tree. "I heard that, Frankie Simmons! Your mother is going to be furious that you're spouting that nonsense about me!"

"But, Ms. Delaney, Mom was the one who said it first!" Frankie yelled down through a gap in the boards.

"Frankie Simmons, you just wait till I get you home!" Karen Simmons yelled up.

"That was Mom!" Frankie said, sounding worried

as he peered over the side and saw his mother among what had turned into a crowd around Gina. "Wow!" he said, sitting back. "Mr. Gallagher, the whole town is down there staring up at the tree house!"

Matt dared a look. Maybe not the whole town, but at least eight people *were* down there—his landlord, Jeb Tywall, Frankie's mother, who was tapping her foot, a few others he didn't recognize, and Gina.

She saw him and gave him a slow, tentative smile.

"So much for privacy," Frankie said from beside him.

It took Matt a few seconds to realize that Frankie's dry comment referred to the group of people who'd followed them and sounded exactly like him. He started laughing—long and loudly. And Frankie, grinning because he'd made a grown man laugh, laughed along with him.

"I'm waiting, Frankie!" Karen Simmons called up again.

"I gotta go." Frankie started to slip over the side, but Matt stopped him.

"Frankie?"

The tousled-haired boy looked over his shoulder.

"Thank you. This may be the sweetest thing anyone has ever done for me." Matt swiped at his wet eyes. "Allergies," he said when Frankie frowned again.

"Oh. You're welcome. You still gonna leave town?"

That was a damned good question. "I don't know. Could you send Miss Delaney up here, please?"

"Aw, no! That was the whole point of the fort, to keep girls out!"

"It'll be fine, Frankie," Matt said reassuringly, keeping his voice low. "I won't let her trick me into anything, I promise."

"Okay," he said disappointedly, "I'll tell her to come up."

He climbed down, giving Matt a minute to think about the tears in his eyes and what he was going to do about Gina. Frankie had reminded him about caring in a major way.

If he stuck with her, did Gina have just as much power to teach him about love?

About a half minute later, Gina appeared in Frankie's place. Holding the ladder, she stared around and frowned at him. "You aren't planning on pushing me off the side, are you?" she asked.

Matt patted the boards next to him, his face unreadable. Gina had heard the deep rumble of his laughter earlier and had hoped Matt could forgive her for interfering in his life. But the blank look on his face now told her that maybe she'd been jumping the gun wishing for that much.

"Okay, okay," she said, climbing over the edge of the floor and sitting down next to him. "I know you're irritated with me—"

"Hold on a minute." Matt knelt and looked over the side of the far wall. What Gina and he had to say to each other was private. "The show's over, folks. Frankie and his brother built a tree house and borrowed a few items for it from the neighborhood, which I'll be returning shortly to the rightful owners. Nothing more to see."

Even Gina could hear the disappointed muttering below as the folks who had followed the chase from their homes started trickling away. Finally, when all she could hear was the chirping of some birds and the rustle of leaves, Matt sat back down and stared at her.

The entire run over, except for when she'd spoken with Mr. Tuttle, Gina had been thinking about how much she wanted Matt in her life, and about why she'd been hiding from anything that faintly resembled love since Mac had died. When she looked back at Matt now, she realized why.

Until now, she hadn't found anyone who really needed her. All her life, except for Mac, she had been pushed out of the way at others' convenience. Her parents had pretty much ignored her unless they were fighting and wanted her to take sides. Her dates didn't seem to miss her when she wasn't with them, and she'd been afraid she was going to get pushed aside when another person came along they *did* miss. Gina hadn't found love because she wanted to be the fire in a man's eyes, an overwhelming passion for him, the other half to his whole.

Now, as she and Matt stared at each other, she finally knew what the intensity meant that was in his eyes every time he looked at her. He wanted her. And she wanted him. The feelings she had for Matt had always been unlike anything she'd ever known— strong and powerful. They made her heart pound and her body yearn for him. He was her passion. Was she his? If she was, could she convince him of that?

"I make a stupid habit of trying to cure every ill I see, Matt, just so people will need me," she said, her words coming in a rush. "I'm very sorry for interfering in your life—but deep inside, you needed your father, you just didn't trust him. But he was a different man then. It's been twenty years, Matt. Do you really think you'll still be the exact same way you are now in twenty years? I hope like all get out you'll be different. Kinder, wiser, less critical."

"Gina?"

Her eyes widening, she shut her mouth.

"I can't say I appreciate the character assessment," Matt said with a tiny grin, "but it's okay about my father. Luke and I have made our peace."

"You have?"

He nodded, and then he reached up and caressed the side of her head, running his fingers through her soft black hair and causing all sorts of feelings of desire to boomerang through her.

"But what about us, Matt?" she asked softly.

"I've been afraid I'd only make a woman as giving and full of love as you miserable because you'd end up wanting a man who can *feel*."

"You've been feeling plenty for me since we made love, Matt, you just won't admit it."

Her simple statement stunned Matt. Was she right? Had this torture he'd been going through all day been because of feelings? This fierce attraction to the woman. The *relief* when he was around Gina, like...like when the minister and his wife had rescued him from the streets and told him they weren't letting him go back. That kind of relief. With Gina, he'd felt like a part of something magical, like he was holding something precious, special and serene, like a tinkling glass ornament on a Christmas tree. With Gina, he felt like someone really cared and thought his life was worth saving—and what she had tried to do for him had been only to save his life.

But were all these things together love?

"What if I can't give you back what you need?" he asked, almost pleadingly. "I don't want to have you, just to lose you."

"I know," Gina whispered, moving over until she was sitting on his lap and wrapping her arms around his shoulders. "I know what that's like, and I know what you've been through. Do you honestly think I could do that to you?"

Slowly, he shook his head. She couldn't, and his subconscious knowledge of that was probably what had kept him from leaving today.

Their lips met in a kiss that was torturous, because of where they were, and the fact that they couldn't take it any further. When they pulled apart, Matt slipped his hands under her shirt, just so he could feel the warmth of her skin, and hugged her closer to him.

"You trusted me," she whispered, "and believe me, I've learned my lesson about interfering. I've never been so worried about anyone as I've been about you in my whole life. I'll never do that again, I promise—"

Abruptly, as she noticed his huge grin, she stopped trying to explain herself. "What?" she asked.

"Don't ever change," he said. "I'm just thinking about how funny it is that opposites attract."

Sighing, she threw up her hands. "I personally don't find anything funny about it. You are the most exasperating man I've ever met, and—"

"And you love me."

"I most certainly do not!" Gina's eyes widened.

"Well, maybe I do. I don't know. But even if I do—which I'm not saying I do, mind you—I am not going to sit here and admit that to you."

"Why not?"

"Because that's not the way it's done."

"I thought it was 'ladies first.'"

She shook her head. "Love is equal opportunity."

"I guess I have a lot of learning to do about love," he told her. "How would you feel about teaching me?"

Gina's mouth fell open, and, grinning, Matt sucked on her bottom lip, which started another long kiss. When he was done, his expression was earnest.

"It's my turn to talk, and I promise after this I'll let you be the talker," he said, and then dodged the playful slap she gave his arm. "Frankie showed me I've been prejudging an awful lot of people. That started when my parents left me and that fiasco happened in the judge's chambers."

He paused to pull her more snugly against him. "Whenever I meet someone," he continued, "I start out by thinking I'm going to get hurt, or that somebody is going to do me wrong. Any relationship that might have developed pretty much goes downhill from there. I realize now I was scared to trust people because I didn't think I was worth loving."

Cupping her face with the side of his hand, he added, "Then you came along. You started caring about me from the first and never stopped...." He buried his face in her hair, not wanting to think what his future might have been like if she hadn't agreed to pose as his wife and changed him.

"So you've forgiven me?" she whispered, half turning in his arms to look at him.

"You and Frankie both." He grinned down at her. "That's some kid, huh? Building this place just for me?"

"Boy, you *have* learned something from all this," Gina said, glancing around the tree house. "But what you don't seem to understand is that he built this place so you could hide from me."

He grinned.

"*I* don't particularly think that was so noble," she said with a sniff.

"You aren't thinking like an eight-year-old boy," Matt said, grinning at her.

"I guess that's true. So if that's the idea of this place, what am I doing up here in its sacred boundaries?"

"You're up here because I'm not thinking like an eight-year-old boy, either," Matt said.

"I guess that means you want me."

He grinned. "I've always wanted you from the second I first saw you, and you know it." He stared into her huge brown eyes. "It's time I put away the past and quit fearing the future, Gina. I started that yesterday with my dad, thanks to you, and now I want to start it with you, if you'll have me in your life."

His face was so filled with the uncertainty and fear that she would say no, that Gina had to reach up and kiss him. And when she did, she knew.

Lightning can strike twice.

Epilogue

➤◆◄

Two months later

"But Mr. Gallagher, you promised you wouldn't let Ms. Delaney trick you into anything!" Frankie said softly enough for everyone in the three front pews of the church to hear. Frankie, Matt and Luke, who was best man, were standing in a small side room next to the sanctuary, waiting for the music to start. The boy was officially an usher, but after escorting a few people to their seats, he'd hurried over to make a last-ditch attempt to convince Matt he was making the mistake of his life.

"This is marriage, for crying out loud," Frankie said. "That means you have to keep her *forever*. My dad says that can get expensive."

"Are you worried about my freedom or my bank account?" Matt asked solemnly, holding back his laughter only with great difficulty as he glanced at his father. Frankie was too preoccupied to notice their amusement.

"Is she going to let you climb up into the tree house? Dad says women have to give you permission for everything, and they're always mad about something.''

"Hey, nobody ever told me that," Matt said, rubbing his chin thoughtfully. "Maybe I ought to reconsider this whole thing, after all."

"And you can never go off alone," Frankie added, just warming up. "I thought you liked your privacy!"

His mother stuck her head in the doorway. "Frankie, don't you dare give Mr. Gallagher any ideas," she said sweetly, smiling through gritted teeth. "You'd best come sit with me—*now*."

"Told you they like to give orders!" Frankie whispered, hurrying after his mother.

Far from calling anything off, Matt thought back over the last two months and how well everything had worked out. After they'd come down from the tree house, he and Gina had decided they wanted to see how things worked between them, considering that he was stationed in Virginia and might be for a while, and Gina had a good life already in Bedley Hills that he didn't want her to give up. So he'd stayed with her the rest of the month until he'd had to report for duty. By then they knew they didn't want to live without each other.

It wouldn't be easy. Because he'd be gone a lot on flights and they'd decided Gina shouldn't have to give up her store, they would have to have a commuter marriage. Gina had already made Chantie her manager so that she'd be free to come to Virginia when he wasn't flying.

But now that Matt had a real home, he found he wasn't all that eager to go flying off, and he was considering other work in the future so he could be a full-time husband. He grinned. Maybe even a father. But come hell or high water, he wasn't running from this love. Gina was everything he wanted—not just in a woman, but in life. He felt like he'd finally come home.

Glancing out the door, he thought it looked like about everyone who would be attending had arrived. So he only had one question now—what was holding up the bride?

At the far side of the sanctuary, through the doors that led to the rest of the church, Gina stood waiting next to Chantie, who was her only attendant.

"Can I say it?" Chantie asked. "Please, let me say it."

"What?"

"I told you so," Chantie said, smirking.

Gina rolled her eyes. "I knew you wouldn't let up just because it's my wedding day. I should have made you wear that yellow chiffon bridesmaid dress—the one that made your skin look sallow."

As usual, Chantie ignored her. "Why aren't we starting, anyway?" she asked cheerfully. "It's past time."

Holding her bouquet, Gina peeked through the door into the church. "Believe me, I'm as eager as you are—"

Chantie giggled at the obvious overstatement.

"But it shouldn't be long now, and then Matt should have what could possibly be the best moment of his life."

Chantie's eyes got big. "You aren't going to *do it* in a church, are you?"

"Chantie!" Gina's mouth dropped open as she whirled around to stare at her bridesmaid. "I wasn't referring to *that.*"

"Well, what could possibly be a better moment for the man than sex?"

Gina smiled mysteriously, then turned back to watch as Matt's mother was escorted into the church and headed toward where her son and her ex-husband were waiting for the ceremony to begin. Despite the fact that she'd vowed not to "fix" people's lives again, Luke had asked her for some help with his marriage. As a client. What she'd told him had apparently worked, because a previously hesitant Mary Gallagher was now considering a trial reconciliation with Luke. It was now up to Matt's father to convince his ex-wife that he had changed.

Any minute now, Matt, Gina thought, every inch of her tingling with happiness as Matt's mother paused outside the door to the room where her son was standing, *and the rest of your life is going to start.*

Matt turned to look through the doorway at the pulpit. The minister was in his place.

"Someone should have signaled a start by now," Matt said to Luke, adjusting his tie nervously. "You don't think Gina left me at the altar, do you?"

"That girl is crazy in love with you." Luke grinned, shuffling his feet and glancing at his watch. "But you're right. It *is* time."

"Shouldn't you go find out if Gina's all right?"

"No need. I already know what's going on."

Matt shifted his weight. Luke was looking very serious, and suddenly he was beginning to worry something might be wrong. "Gina *is* here, isn't she?"

"I saw her with my own eyes earlier. But this isn't about your fiancée. This is about me. I'm afraid I can't be your best man, after all."

Matt felt the old walls start to go up, and he forced them down. He had Gina now, and that would be plenty if his father was about to disappoint him again.

"But," Luke added, suddenly grinning, "I found you a volunteer." He turned. "Mary? You can come in now."

"Mom can't be my best man, Luke," Matt joked halfheartedly. Confused, he watched as a man stepped through the doorway.

Dark-haired, the newcomer was taller and much broader through the shoulders than Matt, but the family resemblance was there in his face, as were the memories. Matt stared. It couldn't be. After all these years...two dreams were coming true on the same day.

"Your mother's and my wedding gift to you, with Gina's full approval," Luke told him. "We found your brother."

Matt blinked, hard, at the burning behind his eyes. Walking quickly forward, he met West halfway across the room, and without hesitation hugged his younger brother to him.

"I searched for years," Matt said, turning back to his father but not letting go of West, feeling as though if he did, the mirage in front of him would disappear. "How...?"

"Luke found me," West clarified.

"I saw him on a television talk show. Seems like your brother's gone and made himself famous."

"Famous?" Matt felt dazed. He couldn't believe he had his whole family back in his life, and Gina as the icing on the cake.

"Just a little bit famous," West clarified, smiling at Matt. "I was pushing my seminars and my book."

"You wrote a book?" Matt's eyes widened in surprise. "What kind?"

"Would you believe—motivational? Follow your dreams, make your life what you want."

"Where were you when I needed you?"

West grinned and looked down at Matt's black suit and gestured outside. "I saw your bride. I'd say you found your dream just fine without my advice."

"I never used to follow it, anyway," Matt quipped back.

"Wasn't that the truth!"

It was like they'd never been apart, Matt thought. West had always been the optimist, the good boy to his bad, the good-humored one who never wanted anyone upset. Life hadn't appeared to have killed his easygoing, happy manner, but knowing what he himself had been through, Matt secretly wondered if West really had escaped their past with no scars. If he had, great. But still...

He nodded slowly at his younger brother. "Your career makes sense. Seminars. You always did like to jabber."

West smirked and punched him playfully on the arm, and Matt jabbed him back and grinned cockily. He couldn't remember ever feeling as good as he did right at this moment. "I don't understand how you turned out bigger than me," he added.

"Must have been all that milk," West said. "You always hated it, so I snuck in and drank yours."

"You did?" their mother asked. "How did I miss that?"

The two of them looked at Mary. "You don't know the half of what you missed, Mom," West said. "We were a pair."

Their mother shook her head and smiled at her ex-husband. "Before I find out something else I don't really want to know, Luke, I think it's time we took our places, don't you?"

Luke nodded. Matt turned to them and gave his mother a quick hug. "Thank you. Thank you both."

They left the room smiling.

Matt had a million questions, but he didn't know where to start. He just stared, almost dumbfounded, at his brother.

"I met Gina," West told him. "You're very lucky."

"I know. How about you?" Matt asked. "You married? Any kids?"

A shadow crossed over West's face.

"Bad subject?" Matt asked.

The shadow disappeared, replaced by the once-again familiar, cocky grin. "We're standing here at *your* wedding, big brother, and you're asking me if marriage is a bad subject? Where'd you find that sense of humor from? You didn't have it when we were kids."

"Must have been Gina." The fact that his brother

had changed the subject wasn't lost on Matt. He stared him straight in the eye and West stared back.

"We should get out into the church before someone decides to take your place," West said. "If you wait any longer, Gina might start thinking we went out for a quick beer and find someone she likes better."

"God forbid," Matt said meaningfully.

"She's that great?"

"She's that great," he replied, totally serious. "Just remember, West," he added, heading toward the door to the sanctuary with his brother a step behind, "I'm here if you need me."

"That was worth waiting twenty years to hear," West said.

The minister saw them enter and signaled the organist to begin. Matt leaned close to his brother to make sure he could hear his next words. "Just do me a favor and don't need me until after the honeymoon's over."

West grinned, and both of them turned just in time to see Gina follow her bridesmaid inside the church. Matt's breath caught and he put his brother totally out of his thoughts. She looked beautiful in her wedding gown, a pearl-studded lace bodice over a white satin skirt. The neckline showed just enough cleavage to remind him of how eager he was to get her out of all that satin and lace. He glanced at the minister as Gina joined him.

After the wedding, of course.

The two of them spent an appropriate amount of time at the reception in Gina's backyard and then slipped away to a hotel room on the other side of town.

Matt picked her up and carried her over the threshold, white gown and all. He had begged her to wear it to the hotel, and even though walking through the lobby had embarrassed her no end, the fact that Matt was looking forward to taking the gown off her gave Gina the courage to go through with it. After the bellboy had left, Matt kicked shut the door and set her on her feet. A second later, their lips locked together in a kiss that rocked her off her heels.

"I take that to mean you enjoyed your surprise?" she whispered, her arms wrapped around his neck.

"My mother enjoying my father's company? Sure."

She shook her head in exasperation. "Having your brother here for your wedding, you nincompoop."

"Is that any way to talk to your husband?" He kissed her again, and added, "Maybe I should have listened to Frankie. He tried to talk me out of marriage, you know."

"Really?" she asked, her fingers unbuckling his belt.

"He as much as warned me I'd never have any privacy again." Matt rained more kisses down her neck to her bare collarbone, while his fingertips ran over the off-the-shoulder lace sleeves she was wearing. There couldn't be anything sexier than lace on Gina, he thought. "Can you imagine that?"

"Hmm, don't worry. I've got that privacy thing covered," Gina said, her head falling back as he worked his lips down to the top of her cleavage.

"You do?" he murmured.

"Uh-huh." She ran her fingers down his chest and slowly, reluctantly, pushed him away. "Let me show you." Walking to her suitcase, she opened the top and took out a lace-trimmed heart. "To hang on the doorknob outside our room," she said, handing it to him. "It ought to keep everyone away."

Do Not Disturb!
Honeymooners In Quarantine.

Matt read the square letters she'd printed and looked up at her. "This won't fool Frankie."

"Of course not." She shook her head. "Him, I had to bribe. But everyone else will leave us alone." Lifting her skirt, she flashed him a view of her thigh-high stockings and silk garter belt. "And we want to be alone, Matt, so hurry up and put out that sign."

Gulping, Matt hurried, triple-locked the door, and returned to her in the time it took her to slip off her pumps and move next to the bed. If his eyes weren't playing tricks on him... "You aren't wearing any panties," he said softly, as he slipped his arms around her.

"I know you wanted to take off my gown, but really, Matt," she said, smiling softly at him, "why waste time?" Pushing him backward so that he fell onto the bed with her in his arms, she helped him with his clothes until it was just him and her and yards of lace and soft white satin.

Matt was in heaven. Crushing her to him, he gave her another long kiss. "So what are we quarantined with?"

"Lovesickness, of course," she said.

"That was what I was hoping you would say," he said, rolling her over onto her back and helping her push the satin up so that he could feel her hot skin and nylons against him.

"Why?" she whispered.

"'Cause I have the cure for what ails us." Lowering his lips to hers, he proceeded to show her exactly what that cure was.

* * * * *

*If you liked THE ONE-WEEK WIFE,
be sure to read about West Gallagher's story
in THE ONE-WEEK BABY, coming July 1997
from Silhouette Yours Truly. Turn the page for
a taste of Hayley Gardner's
next delectable story....*

FOR BETTER...FOR WORSE...
FOR A WEEK!—
the seven days that turned two couples
topsy-turvy!

THE ONE-WEEK BABY

by HAYLEY GARDNER

Dear Mr. Gallagher,

Your book on getting what you want out of life was so awesome, I just had to go to your seminar. That's where you convinced me—I've got to run and lasso my dream while there's still time, just like you told us we should. You were so nice and caring about people's troubles during your class, I know you won't mind taking care of my Teddy while I'm gone. You shouldn't have a lick of trouble. I don't think I'll be gone past Saturday—at least, I hope not. Anyway, with you taking care of Teddy, I won't worry about a thing. I'll be in touch!

Thanks,
Marcia (the checker at The Shopette)

P.S. I sent a copy of this note to my lawyer so she'll know my Teddy's in good hands.

Folding Marcia's note in half, West Gallagher gazed down at the blanket-covered wicker laundry basket on his front porch. How nice, he thought uneasily, that Marcia-from-the-Shopette wasn't going to worry. He, on the other hand, had a feeling he was about to get plenty worried—unless, that was, by *Teddy* this Marcia was referring to her favorite stuffed animal.

But no... Something shifted under the blanket, and the surface rose and fell like an undulating wave. Whatever it was, it could move. Not a teddy bear, then. Maybe a puppy.

Not a puppy. As West stood frozen in place on what had seconds before been his very boring front porch, he knew both guesses were wrong. He knew this because he thought this "Marcia-From-the-Shopette" would probably have taken a puppy or a stuffed bear with her while pursuing her dream. Only children ever seemed to prove a burden for parents when it came to moving on.

That he knew for a fact. Shortly after West had turned eight, his father had left home and not come back, and West distinctly recalled that neither he nor his eleven-year-old brother Matt had been invited to join him. West knew now that either of them tagging along would have just slowed his father down. Marcia had probably left her very own version of a Pandora's Box on his doorstep for the same reason—a child got in the way of personal freedom.

But his father eventually had returned, and West hoped now that just like Luke, Marcia would come back, too, full of remorse, maybe even in the week that she'd promised. West suddenly recalled himself as a little boy clinging to that exact same hope as days, and then weeks went by without his seeing his old man, and then, when everything went out of control, his mother, and then his brother. Clenching his jaw, he forced back the memories. Just because he'd been left alone didn't mean that Marcia wouldn't return for her baby.

Did it?

His gut tightening, West looked up and down the street, hoping for a miracle. But then he heard a gurgling sound and looked down at the wicker basket illuminated in his golden porch light.

Blue elephants appliquéd on the sheet blanket rose and fell, and West knew that no matter how much he wanted to remain in a pleasant, zombielike state of inactivity and denial, there *was* a baby under that cover, and he had to do something. But in that basket was a time bomb, just waiting for him to get close enough so it could explode and disintegrate his perfectly organized life, and he was very reluctant to unwrap the package....

* * * * *

SILHOUETTE... **Where Passion Lives**

Order these Silhouette favorites today!

Now you can receive a discount by ordering two or more titles!

SD#05988	HUSBAND: OPTIONAL	
	by Marie Ferrarella	$3.50 U.S. ☐ /$3.99 CAN. ☐
SD#76028	MIDNIGHT BRIDE	
	by Barbara McCauley	$3.50 U.S. ☐ /$3.99 CAN. ☐
IM#07705	A COWBOY'S HEART	
	by Doreen Roberts	$3.99 U.S. ☐ /$4.50 CAN. ☐
IM#07613	A QUESTION OF JUSTICE	
	by Rachel Lee	$3.50 U.S. ☐ /$3.99 CAN. ☐
SSE#24018	FOR LOVE OF HER CHILD	
	by Tracy Sinclair	$3.99 U.S. ☐ /$4.50CAN. ☐
SSE#24052	DADDY OF THE HOUSE	
	by Diana Whitney	$3.99 U.S. ☐ /$4.50CAN. ☐
SR#19133	MAIL ORDER WIFE	
	by Phyllis Halldorson	$3.25 U.S. ☐ /$3.75 CAN. ☐
SR#19158	DADDY ON THE RUN	
	by Carla Cassidy	$3.25 U.S. ☐ /$3.75 CAN. ☐
YT#52014	HOW MUCH IS THAT COUPLE IN THE WINDOW?	
	by Lori Herter	$3.50 U.S. ☐ /$3.99 CAN. ☐
YT#52015	IT HAPPENED ONE WEEK	
	by JoAnn Ross	$3.50 U.S. ☐ /$3.99 CAN. ☐

(Limited quantities available on certain titles.)

TOTAL AMOUNT	$_____
DEDUCT: 10% DISCOUNT FOR 2+ BOOKS	$_____
POSTAGE & HANDLING	$_____
($1.00 for one book, 50¢ for each additional)	
APPLICABLE TAXES*	$_____
TOTAL PAYABLE	$_____
(check or money order—please do not send cash)	

To order, complete this form and send it, along with a check or money order for the total above, payable to Silhouette Books, to: **In the U.S.:** 3010 Walden Avenue, P.O. Box 9077, Buffalo, NY 14269-9077; **In Canada:** P.O. Box 636, Fort Erie, Ontario, L2A 5X3.

Name:_____

Address:_____ City:_____

State/Prov.:_____ Zip/Postal Code:_____

*New York residents remit applicable sales taxes.
Canadian residents remit applicable GST and provincial taxes.

Silhouette®

SBACK-SN4

And the Winner Is...
You!

...when you pick up these great titles
from our new promotion at your
favorite retail outlet this June!

Diana Palmer
The Case of the Mesmerizing Boss

Betty Neels
The Convenient Wife

Annette Broadrick
Irresistible

Emma Darcy
A Wedding to Remember

Rachel Lee
Lost Warriors

Marie Ferrarella
Father Goose

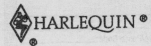

HARLEQUIN ® Silhouette®

Look us up on-line at: http://www.romance.net   ATWI397-R

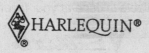

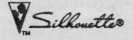